About the Author

Throughout his life, Tyler has loved to write as a form of escape. His aim has always been to take issues he has experienced in his personal life and flush them out in his stories. He hopes to help people gain a better understanding of others' problems through his work, and that readers enjoy the journey through the world that he has crafted.

The Creature without a Voice

Tyler Preneta

The Creature without a Voice

Olympia Publishers
London

www.olympiapublishers.com
OLYMPIA PAPERBACK EDITION

Copyright © Tyler Preneta 2023

The right of Tyler Preneta to be identified as author of this work has been asserted in accordance with sections 77 and 78 of the Copyright, Designs and Patents Act 1988.

All Rights Reserved

No reproduction, copy or transmission of this publication may be made without written permission.
No paragraph of this publication may be reproduced, copied or transmitted save with the written permission of the publisher, or in accordance with the provisions of the Copyright Act 1956 (as amended).

Any person who commits any unauthorised act in relation to this publication may be liable to criminal prosecution and civil claims for damage.

A CIP catalogue record for this title is available from the British Library.

ISBN: 978-1-80074-831-6

This is a work of fiction.
Names, characters, places and incidents originate from the writer's imagination. Any resemblance to actual persons, living or dead, is purely coincidental.

First Published in 2023

Olympia Publishers
Tallis House
2 Tallis Street
London
EC4Y 0AB

Printed in Great Britain

Dedication

To you, Dad. I hope I made you proud.

Acknowledgements

Without the grace of God and the support of Amy, Evan, Srid, Shane, my brother, Michael, and my mother, Lisa, this would have never become a reality. Thank you all. I love you.

CHAPTER 1

I was at Taylor's house when it started. We were upstairs and heard dishes crash to the floor, followed by her mother's scream. As we ran to the top of the stairs, Taylor shouted down and asked if everything was okay. There was no response, only a low gurgle, like someone trying to speak through water. We rushed down the stairs to see Taylor's father standing over her mother. His back was turned towards us when a dark, snake-like ooze dropped from his head and into the mother's mouth. She began violently convulsing before letting out a sharp exhale like she'd been punched in the chest.

"What did you do?" Taylor asked as she ran to her father's side.

There was no answer from him, only a guttural moan. When she looked at his face, she screamed just like her mother. Her father threw his arms into the air and brought them down on top of her head. The blow landed with a crippling thud, and Taylor lay motionless on the floor. He flipped her onto her back and seemed to start giving her mouth to mouth. She had the same reaction as her mother, if not more violent.

I felt like running, but my feet stayed frozen to the floor. Taylor's mother began convulsing again, but only for a few seconds. She rose to her feet, clutching her stomach then her throat, and then her mouth rocketed open. Her cheeks began to rip apart as her jaw smashed down against her chest. That same black tar that had been dropped into her mouth made its way back out, but it wasn't ooze anymore. It came out firm and straight. The substance began snaking back and forth like it was blowing in the wind. She looked at me, tears rolling down her now mangled face. Slowly, the father turned to me and revealed that his face had been ravaged by the same creature. The two of them began walking toward me, whaling with each step. The look of terror and pain on their faces told me that they could feel everything.

"P-Please stop…" I begged, having no idea what else to do, but they kept coming.

I sprinted up the steps and barged into Taylor's room, slamming the door behind me. Her parents caught up and tried smashing their way in. There was a bathroom attached to the room which had a door out into the hall. I bolted into the bathroom then straight to the hallway just as Taylor's parents got into her room. They fell over themselves as they tried to change direction and reach me. I sprinted down the stairs and quickly swung open the front door. Before I could run out, a hand clamped down on my shoulder. I spun to fight it off, thinking it was one of the parents, but it was Taylor. She was crying and holding her stomach. I tried consoling her and thought I could bring her with me, but her jaw unhinged itself and that awful creature slithered its way out. She screamed as it came, but eventually her throat was blocked and all she could do was moan. She grabbed my face with immense strength and tried to open my mouth. The creature hardly moved as it stretched itself towards me. I lifted my knee as high as I could and kicked Taylor in the chest. She stumbled back and dropped me. I turned and darted out the front door just as her parents were making their way down the steps. If only it all ended there.

My name is Alexandria, and the world has ended.

CHAPTER 2

People were turning into those things all over the world. These new monsters were named Pukes, since they constantly looked like they were throwing up. Before all news communications were cut, rumors started popping up saying that there were other variations of the monster, but there was no proof of it. Quarantine zones quickly became enforced, and they were all governed by the military. They set up one around where my family was already living, so we were able to stay in our own home. That lasted for a couple months, until all the ruling bodies of the world fell. After that, there was a mass exodus from the zones in an effort to find a place to survive, but my family decided to stay in our house.

We were all together in my parents' room one night when the sounds of banging and shouting started outside. My father jumped up and ran to the window just as the people came in. They didn't sneak in, like people used to do; they kicked in the front door and started screaming:

"Hello! This is our house now! If anyone is in my home, come out here or die!"

My father used to be a lawyer, so he told us that he could go down and make an agreement. The conversation started relatively pleasant. My father greeted them like friends and they did the same to him. After some talking that I couldn't quite make out, my father yelled. There was a loud bang and the sound of something heavy hitting the floor. My mother's panicked gasp must've attracted the intruders' attention. They started marching upstairs, so my mother slid me under the bed and told me to stay there no matter what.

As she stood up, the people came in. They laughed at her as they shoved her to the floor and started beating her. I covered my mouth to try to stay quiet, but it was so hard. She started to beg for her life, but that just made them taunt her more. I wanted to move, to do something to help her, but I was frozen. As my mother pleaded, her eyes would dart over to me, which they quickly caught onto. One of them walked over and yanked me out so fast I hardly had time to scream. My mother's cries went from begging for her life to begging for mine.

"Sorry," one of the men said, "we are fresh outta space."

I recognized the voice as the same one who had been talking to my father. My eyes were fixated on the man. He had a bald head, scraggly beard, and a small scar under his chin. His cut-off plaid shirt showed a crude tattoo of a black snake. He looked at me and smiled with yellow teeth, and all that rage and hatred I felt a second before flew out of my body. It was like his smile stole it and replaced it with fear and desperation for self-preservation. I stayed there as someone held me and my mother was begging for our lives. There was nothing I could do but stare helplessly.

Another man from the group stood my mother up and tore her clothes off. The group of them laughed at her, but the man smiling at me hollered for them to stop. He walked up to my mother and draped her clothes back over her. He apologized as he walked around her, stopping at her back. He asked to know her name, but as she opened her mouth to speak, he pulled out a pistol and shot through the back of her head.

A human body doesn't fall like people think. It doesn't

dramatically fall to the side or slowly slump down. The body crumbles without grace or caring. A switch is shut off and there is nothing more.

My ears rang and my vision tunneled in on my mother's remains as they splayed out on the floor at my feet. The man said something to me, but I couldn't make it out over my own screams. They lifted me up, smacked me till I was quiet, then carried me down the stairs. Just before they brought me outside, I noticed my father's feet in the kitchen doorway. They were twitching enough to give me hope that he was still alive. I was loaded into the front seat of a rusted truck and driven away by my mother's murderer.

"The world is a wild thing and it goes in cycles. The strong rise up, then something chaotic happens and those who remain, who were crushed for so long, take their place. Over and over again it goes," my mother's murderer said with a small grin. No response came to mind so I continued staring down at my bloody feet. He peeked over at me. "I'm Georgie," he continued, "I'm going to be your new best friend." He bumped me and told me to look at him, but I couldn't muster up the courage. "Look at me!" he demanded as he slammed his fist down onto the center console. My eyes became glued to him, and he showed me that awful, toothy smile. "Good girl... So, what's your name?"

"A-A-Alexand-dria," I stuttered.

He chuckled and patted me on the thigh as he told me how pretty my name was. We spent about an hour driving down cracked and bumpy roads. The cars that used to litter the path were all smashed to bits or flipped onto their side. At times, there'd be people running, walking, or dying on the side of the road, but they were paid no mind. My thoughts raced about where we were going and what was waiting for me when we got there.

Georgie turned down a road bordered by dense woods. He welcomed me home when we arrived at a large brick wall with a small gate to drive through. There were some people gathered around the entrance, and when they noticed the car approaching, they quickly slid it open. Signs along the wall said it was a senior living community, but it was now being used as this group's base of operations.

Being locked inside with these murderers should've scared me, which it did at first, but then I saw who was also there. I saw people walking dogs or sitting in rocking chairs on their porches. It seemed like a chunk of frozen time from before the outbreak. Georgie pulled into a driveway at the very back of the compound and told me to get out. It was a single story house, with cracked, yellow siding.

"This is my place," he said. "Well, our place now."

Georgie pulled me into the house and started giving me a tour. The walls were sky blue and filled with chips and cracks. The lime green couch in the living room stunk of mold, and the wooden table in the kitchen only had three legs. He apologized for not offering me food, but told me that's what the cafeteria was for. There was a scratchy, wooden door at the back of the house that led to a basement staircase. He instructed me to follow him down the creaky steps, and I did so without question. There was a slight dip in one of the steps that threw me off balance. I stumbled down and ended up in his arms.

"Careful," he smiled. "I won't always be there to catch you."

The room at the bottom was coated in moonlight from a small, corner window. A single cot was in the middle of an otherwise empty room made of concrete. Every fiber of my being screamed for me not to listen when he told me to close my eyes, but what choice did I have? He gently twisted me till my back was facing him, then he placed his hands underneath my shirt and traced up and down along my bra. Instinct took over as I spun to face him, crossing my arms in front of my chest.

"You move... when I tell you to move..." he said, his voice almost sweet in tone. Then his balled fist crashed into my stomach, lifting me off my feet. I collapsed to the floor, gagging from the blow. "I need to teach you how to behave."

He forced my body open to him. He responded with a sound of disappointment when I resisted, so he began clubbing me across the face over and over till I passed out. My body was numb when I woke up, except for the space between my legs. The courage it would've taken for me to open my eyes was way too much to ask. I told myself that he was gone and I was alone. The sharp sound of a zipper made me realize I was wrong.

A creek echoed out from the opening door, which closed again after a beat. Once I knew he was gone, reality set in and fear gripped me like never before. A cold sting radiated up my ankle from the chain around it. I felt emotions, but they were all jammed together so not a single one was free. It could've been an hour or a minute, but it felt like an eternity passed before I tried moving again. My fingers traced across the dents and bumps that now covered my face. The moonlight stung my eyes, and as I studied its beauty, my emotions finally showed. I covered my swollen face and wept out of pity and helplessness. I prayed for someone's help, but quickly learned that God's answer is sometimes 'no.'

A few hours passed before the door creaked open again. Georgie was holding a tray of food which he placed in front of me. I had no interest in it. Even if my body wanted to eat, my mind wouldn't let anything pass my lips.

"How old are you?"

"Sixteen," I said, not daring to answer him slowly.

"So in all those years you were with your parents, they didn't teach you to say 'thank you' when you're given something?"

An apology brewed in my mouth, but before it could be said, he struck me across the face, then crumbled away more of my innocence. This happened over and over again for the next few weeks, maybe months. Time seemed like this faraway thing that didn't apply to me anymore.

Eventually all the pain I felt before, during or after Georgie's visits, faded away into a deep pit somewhere inside me. When something is done to someone enough, no matter how terrible, it just becomes their way of life.

One night, on his third or fourth visit of the day, I asked Georgie why he was doing these things to me. As he lifted his weight off me, he looked at me like I was an innocent child asking an obvious question.

"I lead these people. They look to me for guidance," he said softly. "You're my stress relief. I NEED to have a clear head to be able to get through all this. You're the one who keeps my mind like a polished mirror." He paused for a minute but still studied me. "There are two types of people in this world. There are people who sit and wait for something good to happen. Then there are those who claw and drag themselves to the top." He glanced down at his curled fingers. "It has been extremely hard on my nails."

One night, spent, like most others, waiting for Georgie to find a convenient time to visit me, there was an abrupt grinding coming from outside. I figured it was Georgie making his way to me. I turned to the window so he wouldn't punish me for making a face he didn't like, and I noticed a pair of boots outside. Studying them, I could tell they didn't belong to Georgie; they were too small. The stranger knelt, and I saw a woman with beautiful ivory skin. Her gentle smile lit up my room. She put her finger on her lips, telling me to be quiet. She tilted the window open and slid in a set of keys.

"I'm sorry, dear. I should've come sooner," she said, before running from the window.

The keys reflected the cold moonlight back at me, and my body warmed with stress as I thought of leaving. There were at least twenty keys on the ring, so it took some time, but eventually the chain clicked open. My foot had long been asleep so my walking was thumpy and ungraceful. As quickly and quietly as I could, I went into the main house. My own breath seemed enough to interrupt the deafening silence. The front door creaked as it opened. I tried covering my naked body as I stepped outside and saw two sets of boots waiting for me. The woman who was my saving grace was standing alongside my tormentor.

"After all I've given you, you spit in my face by trying to run?" Georgie said before he ripped me inside and threw me back down the basement steps. I screamed in pain, but it didn't seem to affect Georgie. He marched down to me and started beating me. His hands must've grown sore, so he took off his belt and continued his assault on me. That only lasted for a few blows since he must have missed hitting me with his fist, so he wrapped that belt around his hand to provide a little cushion.

He'd battered me before, but this felt different. It was like a spoiled child beating an old toy before throwing it away. But I was okay with finally being thrown away. I wouldn't have to be his play thing anymore, and maybe I'd see my family again. The sounds of vicious punches faded to a monotonous noise like the ocean crashing on the sand. I was at peace. This feeling was something new to me, but it was suddenly interrupted by the ripping clatter of a gunshot. Georgie spun and ran out the door.

Yelling started and was followed by another shot. Georgie stumbled backwards into the door, tumbling down the steps again and clutching his stomach. I thought this was another trap or joke. If I ran out that door, I was going to be beaten again, and this time I'd die for sure, which did give the idea a touch of merit.

    I sat there like a statue, not sure whether I should leave or stay, until a stranger burst in. He picked me up and raced out the door. Pukes had begun flooding in from the entrance and going into homes. That perfect silence was now a cavalcade of pure chaos. A small hoard of Pukes noticed us and started in our direction as the man carrying me sprinted for the exit. I wanted to escape his arms and make a run for it by myself, but I couldn't. My body was too beaten. The darkness closed in on my vision till it was nothing but a silver of sight. I gave into it and allowed myself to pass out in the stranger's arms.

CHAPTER 3

A warmth consumed my body and snapped me awake. As I opened my eyes, I saw the man sitting next to a fire. I tried to move away, but my body was too weak to do much of anything and all my attempt did was alert the man that I was awake. He came over to me, so I clamped my eyes closed and begged for him not to hurt me. There was a long pause before I gathered the courage to look at him. He was sitting on the ground and began moving his hand towards me. My begging intensified as I covered my face and waited for a beating.

"Stop shaking, sweetie. I'm not going to hurt you," he said as he patted me on the head.

He had a gentle smile that coaxed me into dropping my hands. I didn't know what to think about him. Part of me prayed that he was telling the truth, but another part was waiting for his face to twist to one I was more accustomed to. Either way, I had no choice but to trust what he was telling me since I was too out of it to do anything else. Black consumed the corners of my vision till it was all I could see. Just before I dropped out of reality again, I prayed that I'd wake up, but if not, that I at least wouldn't feel what killed me.

The moisture of the morning dew and the piercing light of the sun woke me from my dreamless sleep. There was now a grey, itchy blanket covering me from head to toe. The man was standing across from me, going through two different backpacks. Just as I thought about sneaking off, he started walking over with one of the bags. One was a dirty brown color with a large flap that covered the opening. He told me it was mine to keep and placed it at my feet. When I sat up, I noticed that I was dressed. My throat ached – it had been ever since I'd met Georgie – but I was able to eke out a 'thank you' as he headed back to his bag.

"Do you want your blanket back, mister?" I asked him.

"No, sweetie. That's yours now. Fold it up and put it away in your bag," he replied. "Oh, and the name is Donnie."

A sheepish smile grew across my face as I told him my name was Alexandria, but that my friends called me Alex.

"Okay, Alex," he said with a smile. "Let's get moving."

My hands screamed in pain as I went to fold the blanket. Donnie walked over to me once I'd dropped it more than a few times and looked over my arms. They'd been sliced from the fall down the steps and my attempts at self-defense. He cursed as he ran over to his bag and brought back bandages. Pouring alcohol onto a cut isn't really what hurts; it's when you stop pouring and let it soak in that the pain truly starts. Before, Georgie's punches would normally make my vision go fuzzy, and the other things he'd done to me were justification for my feeling that I likely wasn't meant to be in this terrible world. All I'd felt in a long time was fear and helplessness, so it was nice to feel the sting of alcohol cleaning my wound and healing what was left.

After Donnie finished wrapping me up, he gave me a pat and told me to get familiar with what was in my bag: a flashlight, some old sticks, newspapers, a canteen, and a folding knife. I gingerly reached in for the knife, trying to not alarm Donnie. Distrust and suspicion are hard instincts to shake, so having a knife in my hand would make me feel a bit more at ease, even if I wasn't sure if I could actually use it. After going through his bag for some time, Donnie took out a pistol and put it in a holster on his hip. Staring at the weapon, I thought that it may be used to kill me. Thankfully, there wasn't much time to let my thoughts fester because, after he holstered the gun, he gestured for me to follow him. The thought of running dashed through my mind like a roaring train. I'd have loved to escape and go back home, where maybe someone who I used to know would still be alive, but I knew that would likely be my death sentence. Even if I ran, I had no knowledge of how to make shelter, get food and water, or fight. I'd become abandoned in a world already lost. Following Donnie was my only real option, but I held my knife firmly and my mind rang loud with prayers.

We walked down a main stretch of road, keeping the woods at our side. There was silence as we walked. I'm sure he felt as awkward about the situation as I did fearful.

"You know," he said, cutting the silence like a hot knife through butter, "if I wanted to hurt you, I would've done it already." This brief mention of violence shot a chill up my spine. As nonchalant as I could, I placed more distance between us. "What I'm saying is that you don't have to be afraid. I just want to help you," he continued.

Nodding, I said, "I understand," but there was no way I was letting my guard down.

It's amazing how quickly nature had overtaken the man-made structures of earth. It was like a bank coming to collect on a loan, or a mother taking away her child's toy because he hadn't done his chores. The world was no longer a paradise of brick and metal, but a wonderland of wood and vines. We ended up finding an abandoned gas station that embodied this perfectly: trees grew from inside, plant life crawled up the walls and signs, and small animals had made it their home.

Donnie told me to jump through one of the smashed

windows, but I wasn't sure if I wanted to. He'd been nothing but kind so far, but the idea of me and him alone in a dark building didn't sit well with me. He jumped in and looked back for me to follow. My feet felt fixated to the ground as I thought of an excuse to not go in with him.

"You know, if you'd feel better, you can open up the knife," he called out, smiling and continuing to wait.

I brought my knife out from behind me and opened it. The pop of the spring as it flew open scared me and almost made me drop it. Donnie let out an exaggerated laugh, like a dad laughing at one of the jokes only he thought was funny, then waved me in to join him.

I hopped through the window, knife at the ready, and stood beside Donnie. He told me to go and search one section of the gas station while he searched the other.

"Oh," he said loudly, "it's always a good idea to find more than one exit, just in case." I nodded to him and moved to my side of the store.

The sign for 'food' drew my attention directly to it. That turned out to be a loose term since most of the stuff left over wasn't edible: some moldy fruits, cans of dog food, and torn open cereal boxes were all that was left. I headed over to Donnie to let him know about how little I'd found. He was searching along the small, refrigerated section, where all I could see was curdled milk and melted ice creams.

"There was nothing on my side," I told him.

"Don't worry, there's always something," he said. "You just don't know how to look."

We walked back over to my side so I could show him the remains. Donnie looked at me and smiled. He knelt down, grabbed a can of dog food and the ripped open cereal, and then placed them into his bag.

"But it's all expired," I told him, but he just shook his head. "Now isn't the time to be picky, kiddo."

After placing everything that he called 'edible' into his bag, Donnie brought me back to where he was searching and asked me to find what was useful. Walking up and down the few sections, I found nothing that looked useful at all. When I told him, he pointed towards the very last section which was labeled as 'ice.' The cabinet looked disgusting, with green, yellow and black things growing all over the inside. Upon closer inspection, I noticed a bag that was laying on top of the broken glass and was filled with water. That would've been amazing had there not been dark specks floating in it. When I pointed it out to Donnie, he told me that was a small issue. We cut the bag with my knife and started to fill our canteens. I was so happy when I realized that there would be water left in the bag. I rolled it up tight and went to place it in my backpack, but Donnie stopped me.

"We have everything we need," he said. "We don't know if someone else may need it." Unenthusiastically, I agreed with him and placed the bag back in the warm cooler.

He opened his mouth to say something, but muffled moaning erupted from the front of the station. Donnie and I huddled together beneath the window we'd jumped in through. He inched his head up to check if there was anything he could see, but quickly rushed back. His finger was over his lips just as the shadow of a Puke stretched in over us. He pulled out his gun and I clutched my knife, but all I could do was sit there in fear and try not to breathe. My mind raced as one of them grazed its arm across my head. Immediately, my body tensed, and my feet got under me, ready to run, but Donnie stopped me. He grabbed my thigh and whispered, "Stay calm." There was a broken bottle on the floor that he had me hand to him. After a momentary pause, he lobbed it over the Pukes and it crashed on the concrete outside. The Pukes rushed over to investigate the noise while we climbed out the window. We were able to make it to the tree line without alerting them, then we ran back into the woods.

The Pukes' moans intensified as we ran over dead leaves. We sprinted for a few minutes until Donnie finally told me to stop. My chest was on fire and my feet felt weightless. I flopped onto the ground, while he stood over me to keep watch.

"Scary, huh?" he asked, sitting down next to me.

"Of course it was," I told him, looking at him like he had seven heads. "One of them even touched me."

"Interesting," he responded, as if I had just given him a new math formula. "If it touched you, it should've known that we were there, but it didn't... So if the human part touches you, the monster doesn't feel it!" He looked at me and smiled like we'd won something, but it definitely didn't feel that way.

It took a little more time for me to catch my breath completely, then we continued walking. "I forgot to breathe," I told Donnie, "I got so scared that I... I forgot I needed to breathe." He looked like he understood what I was saying.

"It happens. But if we get cornered again, breathing is at the top of the priority list," he said, smiling, and I smiled back.

My arm was stiff and painful, even as it hung at my side. I checked to see if anything was broken, but noticed it was because of the deadly tight grip I had on my knife. I looked at Donnie, and he looked back at me and the knife before turning his back to keep walking. I used my other hand to pry open my fingers, then folded up the knife and placed it into my pocket. Donnie seemed genuine about not wanting to hurt me, and I believed him enough to not need my knife out constantly. But that didn't mean my hand was going to move from inside my pocket anytime soon.

CHAPTER 4

Darkness began overtaking the sky, and Donnie suggested that we camp somewhere close. There was a clearing between the trees that looked perfect to me, but Donnie disagreed. He suggested we find a place that offered more shelter instead of being out in the open, so we trudged on. We cut through part of the woods and back onto a road just as it began to rain. My body craved rest, so when Donnie saw a large office building that we could sleep in, I ran towards it joyfully, with a complete disregard for my surroundings. A quick tapping of feet followed inches behind me. I thought it was funny how Donnie didn't seem to mind if we went all night to find a place, but now that we had, he was running right along with me.

"Didn't seem like you'd be this excited," I joked as I turned around. It wasn't Donnie. It was a man covered in a throbbing black spider web that came from his mouth. Only a few bits of skin and ragged clothing peeked through. His eyes had rolled back, showing only their white underbellies. My legs cramped as fear overwhelmed me and forced me to stop. Slowly, as if not to frighten me, the monster reached its arm towards me. Donnie shouted for me to move as he shoved me to the side and shot the creature several times. It smashed onto the ground and let out a high-pitched hiss, like the sound of water boiling in a kettle. I was cemented in awe as I studied the creature, but Donnie pulled me out of it. He hoisted me over his shoulder and charged inside the building.

"What are you doing?" he hollered. "I yelled for you to run, but all you did was stand there! You have to listen to what I tell you to do!"

My eyes filled with tears as I realized how terribly afraid I'd become. I went to apologize, but before I was able to let a single word out, Donnie grabbed me and hugged me tight. Even more fear and anxiety flooded though my body as he gripped me. My body twitched for him to release me, but he didn't. I started throwing violent punches and kicks in all directions in an attempt to get him off. He pinned my arms at my sides and told me that I needed to calm down. Looking at him again, I realized that I wasn't with Donnie. I was back in the room with Georgie on top of me. I hadn't gone anywhere.

The stinging cold from my chains began twisting around my legs. Screaming and crying was my only defense, so I began begging for him to let me go.

"You know I can't let you leave," Georgie said with a chuckle.

He let go with one hand, so I braced my body for the inevitable impact. His hand gripped my face, then he moved his fingers to my clamped-shut eyes. Forcefully, he pried them open and told me to look at him. My eyes darted around the room, like they were following a house fly, until they came to focus on him. It was Donnie again, telling me to calm down. He loosened his grip a little more so I was able to rip away from him. I ended up in the corner of the room with my face buried into my hands and an irresistible urge to tremble.

"I'm sorry, sweetie," Donnie said from across the room. "I'm not going to hurt you…"

I pressed my knees to my chest and fell to my side in an attempt to collect myself. Donnie didn't say another word to me.

He was busy building a fire in the middle of the room. There was a massive hole in the top of the roof for the smoke to escape out of. The sound of the rain tapping on the tiled office floor made my tight muscles grow loose and heavy. Then, my eyes betrayed my anxiety as they drooped closed.

I saw my father standing in the middle of my house, asking why I forgot about him so quickly. He yelled that he'd still be with me if I wasn't so selfish with my own life. That if I had any sort of backbone, I would have jumped from Georgie's arms and he'd have been able to hug me again, or maybe I'd be saved from the misery to come. I tried to tell him he was wrong, that I would never forget him, and I'd search for him. He laughed and told me to hurry up and die so that my mother would have company. My body jolted awake and I sat up to study the room. It was still dark out, and Donnie was sitting by the blazing fire, looking over at me.

"Hey, kiddo," he said softly. I felt like a guilty child as I tiptoed over to sit next to him. He asked if I'd had any dreams. I told him that I didn't remember. "That's probably for the best. Dreams now don't tend to be happy ones."

"I… I'm sorry about… before," I said after a long time listening to the crackle of the fire.

As I went to apologize again, Donnie interrupted and told me that there was nothing to be sorry for. He looked at me with a gentle smile across his face and told me to get some more rest. When I asked if he was going to sleep too, he said that he needed to keep watch.

The next morning came and we left as soon as the sun began to rise. The creature was still lying outside the building. Corroded valleys covered the body in the spaces where the black substance had been. I was able to see into the person's body, all the way through to their decaying organs and cracked bones.

"They're called Creeps, and they're what comes after the Pukes," Donnie said. "Once the body of the human host cannot be sustained by the creature anymore and dies, the creature recedes inside. It turns the body into something like a cocoon. Then it explodes out and covers the body in a web of itself. A Creep only needs to touch your face and that is enough to turn you into a Puke."

"That's awful…" I said. Donnie looked down at his feet and nodded in agreement.

That whole day was spent walking along dismantled roads. We'd stop to look through a few abandoned houses, but always made sure to leave something useful behind, which seemed to me like an extraordinarily odd rule for the end of the world. There was one house we came upon that had the front door kicked in. Not knowing if someone or something was still inside, Donnie drew his gun and told me to wait for him outside. There were a few shots before he popped his head back out and told me it was okay to go in.

The house was dated on the inside, which told me that old people had lived there before all this. It made me question how long they'd been able to last, or if they'd lasted at all. My thoughts of the inevitable were interrupted when my foot kicked into the side of a dead Puke's head. The black creature had left the person's mouth and littered the ground like a pile of ash next to them. Their eyes were still open, staring up at me. I wondered if they could still see me. I bent over to inspect it closer, but Donnie called out to me. He said we didn't have time to waste and that we needed to search the house.

As usual, I took one side of the house while he took the other. I was sure that the door being kicked in meant there would be nothing useful left, but it turned out I was wrong. In a back room, there was a small stockpile of food, mostly canned beans. I stuffed it all into my bag then left the room.

The rest of my side didn't have anything else useful, so I headed back to find Donnie. I hollered for him, but there was no answer. A bright yellow door was cracked open and I was able to make out part of Donnie's figure standing in the doorway. Walking in, I saw him standing motionless, staring down at a thick bundle of rope in his hand. I asked if he'd found anything, but there was no response. I crept over to him, not knowing if he was okay or not, and touched him on the arm.

"Oh, hey. Sorry, I didn't hear you come in," he said as his head snapped up to face me. There were beads of sweat running down his forehead and dripping onto the rope. When I asked why he didn't answer me, he said he was lost in his thoughts.

He told me he'd had no luck on his end, but asked if I'd found anything. I pulled out can after can of the food I'd just found and the smile that grew across my face hurt my cheeks. Donnie seemed really pleased until he asked where I'd found it. The smile became twice as painful when it vanished as I realized I hadn't left anything behind. He called me out for it, and I apologized for completely forgetting to leave something. He told me it was nothing to worry about but I could tell it did make him slightly angry.

"The world's gone to shit. Doesn't mean our humanity needs to go too," he said, pulling a few cans out of my bag to leave on a small table.

We headed back outside and continued walking down the same busted up road for a few hours. The further we traveled, the more the question of where we were going boiled in my mind. I decided to ask, and he told me we were going south. I thanked him for being so clear and specific but wanted to know if he could tell me exactly where. After a small chuckle, he said we were going to a rumored safe haven. Somewhere that society hadn't completely fallen apart. This place still had forms of government, and the people living inside were constantly guarded. It was the civilized world's restart point. It was a paradise.

The air was thick and felt warm against my skin as the sun began to set. We found a crumbled house that had a small shed in the back that we decided to stay the night in. My feet were rubbed raw from all the walking, so I threw my bag off my shoulders and plopped onto the ground. Donnie scooped my pack back up off the floor and began patting the dirt off. He started telling me to be careful with it, when I could be, since the stuff inside could save my life.

He said he wanted to show me how some of the stuff could be used to make a fire. Thinking I was a step ahead of him, I reached into my bag and brought out some of the small, dry sticks. He seemed pleased that I knew where to start, but he also pulled out some of the old newspapers.

"It's easier to get a fire started on this, then transfer it over to the sticks," he said. "After the sticks are lit, we can add bigger pieces of wood to it."

Donnie told me to open the shed door and dig a hole for the fire to sit in. He said if we needed to hide, we could cover it. After I dug the hole, Donnie asked for my knife and held out his hand. It was still in my pocket, but I wasn't sure about giving it over to him. I took it out, popped the blade open and looked up at Donnie.

"It's something cool," he said.

Suddenly, the realization hit me that all this time he wanted me to feel comfortable enough so I wouldn't fight back. He wanted to use me just like Georgie did. I quickly made up my mind. I wouldn't let that happen again. I was going to plunge my blade into his stomach as he came close. I shut my eyes and my arms became coiled like a spring. If I couldn't kill him, I'd turn the blade back on myself. I was not letting it happen again. A deep breath was all I needed before thrusting my arms forward. When it struck him, he made a sound like a toad. His hands gripped my face and scratched at my arms, but it didn't bother me. He was dead, and I was safe.

"Thank you," Donnie said in a clam voice as he took my blade.

My eyes slowly opened and the true world came into focus again. He showed me his gentle smile while holding the knife in his hands. He untwisted the hilt till a small piece of metal fell out. After he took that, he folded the blade in and tossed it back to me. My body wouldn't stop shaking.

He broke some sticks and threw them into the hole, then lightly balled up the newspaper and used the metal, which he told me was called flint, to create a spark. It took a few minutes of him trying, but eventually one of the sparks landed on the newspaper. Donnie got really close to it and started blowing. Not like he was trying to blow out a candle, more like he was whistling without the noise. He sat up a bit and I could see the smoke starting to billow. He placed it down into the hole and started stacking small sticks around it.

"There we go," he said while standing up and looking happy as the fire started to glow. "Now it's your turn."

The sound of his boot kicking out the newborn fire made my heart skip a beat. When I asked what the hell he did that for, he told me it was my turn to show what I learned. I took the flint from him and went to try to make a fire. An eternity later, a spark landed on the paper and I blew on it. My breath was no stronger than a baby's laugh. It was just strong enough to get the fire to catch onto the paper, and it lasted long enough for me to transfer it over to the twigs in the hole. Donnie went and collected sticks to pile them on top, until the entire hole was blazing with beautiful fire.

"We should go and grab some more wood to keep the fire going," he said.

Thick brush exploded from behind the shed, and I marched through it to find sticks that were dry and would burn. A massive heap of perfect sticks was piled just a few feet from the door. Approaching it, I noticed something odd; a small foot poking out from under the pile. Clearing the brush away, it revealed itself to be a baby doll. Just the sight of it made me smile. It looked just like the one I'd used to play with. It had peach fuzz hair, pink and purple striped clothes, the prettiest green eyes, and little pink booties on the feet. Mine used to be named Amy, so that's what I named this one.

I brought the firewood and Amy back to Donnie. I was so happy about the doll, but when I showed Donnie, his shoulders rounded and his posture sunk. When I asked what was wrong, he said, "No, nothing... Everything's good. It just surprised me is all."

His tone was happy, but his voice was thin. He asked what I wanted to do with it, and I told him I was going to keep it. I already named it and saved it so I couldn't just get rid of it. Besides, it made me feel as close to happy as I had for a long time, if not a little bitter about the world too. I walked over to my bag and placed it inside.

The rest of the night was spent gazing into the fire. Silent and peaceful moments had been fleeting, so I enjoyed it while I could. Donnie's eyes kept darting toward me, then away from me, as if there was something on his mind that he wouldn't say.

"You okay, Donnie?" I asked, feeling somewhat awkward from his snapping eyes.

"I'm so sorry about what happened before... with Georgie," he said, meeting my gaze.

It's really strange the way certain people act when the tragedy that they try so hard to forget is brought to the forefront of their attention. Some run, or fight, but me, just hearing Georgie's name, I shut down. Death is the end of living, right? So, I must've died with Georgie on top of me. The person I was had died, or maybe they just ceased living.

"It's nothing you need to apologize for... You didn't do anything wrong," I told him.

It was sweet, maybe a little off-putting too, but Donnie's eyes began to well with tears. I wanted to say something, but I had no clue what to say that would calm him. As I wondered how to respond, he said goodnight and pulled his blanket over his face.

"Thank you, Donnie," I said before rolling over and falling asleep.

My parents were in the kitchen on a Sunday morning, cooking French toast before we had to leave for church. Dad was laughing at a crappy joke he'd just made, and mom was looking at him with loving disgust. They both stopped, looked at me as smiles ate their entire faces, then said, "We're dead."

I snapped awake just as Donnie began shaking me. He hunkered down and put his finger to his lips. The door to the shed was closed, and Donnie's boot was covered in ash and dirt. The fresh sunlight peeked through the bottom of the door and showed figures moving in front of it. The sounds they made started out as distant hums, but they gradually began to get closer. They were voices, human voices. They were talking about finding food and supplies soon or they would be in serious trouble.

I asked if we were going to talk to them, but Donnie shook his head no, which was perfectly fine with me. That changed when I heard one of the voices talk about food and utter the word 'muffin.' It was my father. I knew it was. That was exactly what he used to call me, and he said it in that exact way. There was no mistaking it, that was my father. I looked over at Donnie and told him, but he insisted that I stay. He said I couldn't know for sure, but I did. I knew that was him and I needed to follow, even if Donnie wasn't coming. When I told him that, he sighed, rolled his head till it cracked each way, and said he wouldn't let me go alone.

CHAPTER 5

Our footsteps were quiet as whispers, and our breathing was as tight as a vice as we followed the group of men to wherever they were going. They were all walking casually, so I knew that the place they were headed to was close. There were three men in the back, all wearing torn up tee-shirts, ripped camo pants, and boots. My father was leading them. He was just the right height, had my dad's curly black hair, and talked just like him. Knowing I was going to see my dad again filled me with excitement, to the point where I just wanted to run and jump into his arms. The only thing stopping me was Donnie's sense of cautiousness.

The sun was almost at its highest point by the time the men reached their destination. It was a small convenience store with boarded up windows and people standing on top holding rifles. Once they saw the men approaching, the people standing on the building quickly ran down to let them in. Donnie and I were able to reach the building without being seen, since the people on the roof stayed inside. We could only count eight in total: three women and five men, all stood in a circle, talking. I couldn't see my father's face, but I could see his back as he threw his arms in the air. Their words were mumbled but one thing was clear: they were all upset over something. I assumed it was because the men we had followed there hadn't found anything useful.

After some more banter, a woman held a knife up to my father and started screaming that he had no clue what he was doing and that they should just get rid of him. How dare she scream at my dad like that. He never did anything without trying his hardest and I knew that was still true now, even with the world how it was. I told Donnie that we had to go in and help my dad, but he wanted to wait and watch some more. My dad had a knife pointed at him, and Donnie didn't seem too upset by it, so I refused to sit around any longer.

I ripped away from Donnie and burst through the door, demanding that they leave my father alone. Throwing myself between him and this woman's blade was the only thing I could think of to defend him. He placed his hand on my shoulder and squeezed. It felt so good to be with my dad again. He must've felt the same excitement I did, because he was gripping my shoulder really hard. Understanding how he felt, but in pain from his grasp, I turned to hug him. He looked different than what I remembered. His joy and luster were gone, replaced with a dirty, aggressive face. This man was not my father.

My expression became a mangled mess of fear as I tried backing away from the group, only to find my back against the wall. My body felt like the building rested on my shoulders, making me slump to the floor. The group started moving closer to me, asking each other if I was the one, then the gunshots started. I closed my eyes since I thought they were trying to shoot me, though with terrible aim. Donnie's voice began screaming for me to move. He ran into the store and started blasting these people dead. Two women and three men dropped before anyone knew what was happening, the first being my false father. The ones still standing took cover and began firing back. My ears hissed like they'd sprung a leak, so whatever Donnie was yelling for me to do, I couldn't understand. The flashes of murderous light were mesmerizing, almost beautiful in a strange way.

A shadow loomed over me and I thought that I'd feel what

one of the flashes felt like, but nothing happened. Almost impatient for the inevitable to happen, I looked up to see my murderer, but instead of a human, it was a small hoard of Pukes. They crumbled through a window above me with as much grace as a baby learning to walk. I managed to move my stubborn body out of the way before they could crush me. One of the men began screaming that they'd entered the store, and everyone turned their fire towards them. Two of the last three people and Donnie were firing at the Pukes, but one of the others snuck behind Donnie and put a knife to his throat. He hollered for me to help him as the man dragged him to the floor. Under the still-raining fire of the others, I crawled toward him. Donnie's gun was on the floor in a puddle of blood and brain. I scooped it in my arms and made my way to Donnie.

He was scrambling on the floor with the man who'd put him there, and eventually got pinned on his back. The man used his body weight to try and plunge a blade into Donnie's chest. Once Donnie saw me, he started screaming for me to shoot. I thought of it like taking a picture, just point and click. I aimed the sights on the man's hip and pulled the trigger. He was supposed to stay in the same position till after I shot, but that didn't happen. He moved as I fired, and the bullet tore through the left side of his head just as his eyes met mine. Bodies aren't graceful when a bullet tears through them. He crumbled down on top of Donnie, who then threw him off and came for his gun. He placed his blood covered finger over my lips as he made his way to the remaining people shooting the Pukes.

They must not have had any idea what happened behind them, or thought Donnie was already dead, because they didn't even turn back to look. The woman said she was going to check that all the Pukes were dead, and she told the man with her to look around for me. She turned her back on the store, and as the man came around a corner, Donnie sprung up and slit his throat from ear to ear, then jammed the knife in his skull. The woman yelled that everything was clear just as Donnie moved behind her.

"Thanks," Donnie said as he placed the barrel of his pistol to her temple and pulled the trigger.

Blood sprayed from her skull like foam from a shaken champagne bottle. My eyes hurt from how wide they were, and how firmly focused they were on Donnie. He didn't seem affected by his actions. All he did was wipe the blood from his face and kick the body that had landed at his feet to the side. When he started coming towards me, I wanted to move but was only able to sit there, motionless.

My ears rang so loud that it felt like my head was going to explode if it didn't stop. I squeezed my eyes closed, but all I could see was my mother's splattered head. The saying that I was no better than the people who killed her screamed louder than the ringing. I begged for it to stop, but it wouldn't. I threw my head from side to side, but still it continued. I yelled one last plea, but it didn't stop. Just when I felt my ears were going to run off my skull, there was a sharp sting across my cheek. I opened my eyes, even though my head was pounding with pain, and saw Donnie standing over me with his hand flat.

"W-w-why did you k-kill them...?" I asked, feeling my body begin to tremble. "Why d-did I kill her?"

"You have to stay safe with me," he said as he brought out a cloth to clean my face. "They were a threat to you, and I removed that threat. Same thing you did for me."

My mind had just started wrapping itself around Donnie's words, when I looked over to the people he'd just killed. The blood splatter looked extremely familiar to me. One of the bodies was laying in the doorway and we needed to step over it to leave. Their muscles twitched, but that was from the bullet wound in their head. One of the people had their scalp laid to the side like an opened can. It was like someone had loosened a valve that let reality sink into me. The inside of my skull itched as my emotion hit me. I wept for my father's death.

Donnie had me wait by the door while he looked through the store. He found a good stockpile of food inside. We took almost all of it, just leaving behind some chips and peanuts. Once he had it all packed into his bag, he came to me with a childish and gleeful smile.

"As good a time as any to celebrate," he said, while holding up a bottle of whiskey.

With stuttered words, I suggested that we leave since there must've been more Pukes coming after all the gunfire, and Donnie agreed. My mind was racing and my body was exhausted. Donnie would speak to me, but I'd zone out then ask him to repeat himself well after he'd finished. This happened over and over again until he finally stopped talking. Honestly, it's not like I was able to truly understand a word he said because my mind was so focused on the dead bodies, mostly the one I'd killed. Just a second's difference and I wouldn't be a murder, but now, I wondered if I was just like Georgie. Maybe not as bad, but isn't that relative? That man might have had a family who were waiting for him to come home, and I'd ruined that. In a way, I could be worse than Georgie already. Trying to push it away just made it louder, and I just wanted to try and get some sleep.

Hours of walking passed before we found a rundown house in the middle of a field that was good enough to stay the night in. Donnie told me to check one side while he checked the other, but I couldn't bring myself to do it. I told him it was because I was tired and afraid of missing something, but the truth was that I was terrified of being alone with my head.

Everything on the lower floor was clear, and we even found a few cans of food and a fireplace. We crept upstairs and saw three doors lining the hall. I opened one, which led to a bathroom with nothing useful in it. By the time I turned around, Donnie was entering the third door. I ran up next to him, but a gust of thick, humid air knocked me back. Inside, the room was completely black, with only a sliver of light coming from the covered windows. The smell hit me next. It was the smell of decay.

Donnie didn't seem to mind as he stared in at the far corner. I went to pull him out but he shrugged me off and walked into the room. Covering my face, I ran in behind him to find that the thing he was so focused on was a body. It was a girl, only a few years older than me, sitting on the ground. There was a bottle of pills resting in one hand and a bottle of alcohol in the other. Her appearance infuriated me. She looked so calm.

Donnie walked over to her and started to lift her head. He struggled to move her as her body creaked and cracked, but he didn't stop. I started walking toward him just as the girl's head snapped up. Her eyes were crusted closed, her mouth hung open, and her skin was a shade of violet. Vomit ran down her chest and into her long, blonde hair, then spread out on the floor. A few minutes of silence passed before Donnie looked back at me and said he was going to bury her. She was stiff and wouldn't unbend from her sitting position as Donnie lifted her. I ran to help him but he snapped at me to stay away. He took a breath and told me that my job was to clear the way.

I opened the front door and started to go out, but Donnie stopped me and asked that I make a fire. His red eyes and downturned face told me to give him some space. I headed inside, leaving the door open behind me just in case something happened, and started on the fire. It was pretty incredible how easy it seemed now. Just as I was feeling happy for my accomplishment, I heard Donnie muttering outside.

As I was walking out to check on him, he was coming in. He smiled when he saw me, but his face was ruby red and his eyes were swollen. We sat in front of the fire together, and I told him it was nice that he'd taken care of the girl. He responded with a silent nod and smile before digging in his bag. I scooted closer to see what he was looking for, but before I could help, he pulled out the bottle of whiskey. It opened with a crack and a pop, then Donnie placed it to his lips. Swig after swig flooded from the bottle and down his throat like water. I wanted to ask him about what happened at the convenience store, or about the girl upstairs, but he seemed too happy to have any of that brought up. A while was spent silently listening to the fire and intermittent gulps. My eyes grew heavy, but Donnie spoke and snapped me from potential sleep.

"I used to have a bunch of cats, like a mountain of them," he said. I wasn't exactly sure what to say, so I just nodded and said how cool that was. "You know what they call a mountain of cats…? It's a MEOWtain!" I chuckled, not knowing what else to do, but he threw himself into laughter like his joke was the funniest thing he'd ever heard. "Oh boy, I'll tell you, the place we're headed is beautiful… My family is there now, actually."

It surprised me to hear that he had a family, let alone that they were still alive. I asked why he hadn't gone with them. He said it was because he had unfinished business around here, then he took another long drink. He asked if my family was still alive, and I told him that they weren't.

"Well, that's okay," he said. "We have each other now. We're family."

It was difficult to smile after he said that since it seemed like he'd scooted past my family's death. I agreed with him just to move on, then paused for a bit before asking about the convenience store. I wanted to know why the man had sat up when he did. He took another drink before saying that shit happens that we cannot control. There was so much more I wanted to ask, but he gave me a quick goodnight and rolled onto his side.

I curled up on the floor and thought of the way the man's head had exploded from my bullet. When the burn in my eyes became more painful than I could take, I finally let them rest. My parents were standing before me and I wrapped my arms around them. Once we were hugging, they pulled back and called me a murderer, before their heads popped like firecrackers.

I snapped awake to see Donnie passed out next to me with two empty bottles resting at his side. He reeked of throw up and blood. He was in a peaceful-looking sleep, but the sun was starting to peek through the trees, so it was time for us to get moving again. Shaking him didn't do anything other than make him peek open his eyes, mumble a bit, then roll over again. Just as I began thinking I'd need to drop my bag on his head to get him up, he started gurgling and moaning something. It was the same thing over and over again, and even though I couldn't put it together completely, I was almost positive he was mumbling someone's name. When I went to answer his call, his eyes sprung open almost as quickly as he sat up.

"Hey... Morning, kiddo. You good?" he asked, as if I'd been the one sleeping.

I told him he'd been calling out for something, but he just

laughed at me like I'd told a joke. He stood up slowly and rubbed his temples. I asked if he was okay, and he brushed me off saying the wooden floors were to blame. Once we stepped outside, the stench almost made me gag. Under a tree at the corner of the house lay the girl's decaying body. She went from a light violet to a deep dark purple. Donnie stared for a moment before we headed out.

CHAPTER 6

We walked for a long time after that and only stopped at some abandoned stores and gas stations. I was able to think and realize how useless I was. My parents had died when I could've done something, Donnie was almost killed because of me, but instead, I ended up a murderer. Everything I'd ever done had only led to more grief and misery. I knew I needed to change that.

Eventually, we came upon a Super Shop. It used to be a massive store with a bunch of stuff like food, outdoor supplies, clothes, and pretty much anything else someone could want. Donnie gave me a pat and said we were going to look around inside. Pukes, Creeps, thugs, and murders were all potential dangers waiting on the other side of the doors. I tried telling him I wasn't sure about going in, but he told me we'd be fine as long as we were quick.

The front doors had to be forced open to get in. The dirt, blood, and black sludge glistened, reflecting the shine of our flashlights. Donnie told me to check one side while he checked the other. I didn't feel good about that. I asked him to come with me, but he rubbed his head, groaned, and told me that we could be done faster if we did what he wanted. Unenthusiastically, I agreed.

I tried to search like a thief in the night: in quick and out quicker. Donnie was sloppy and loud to the point where I could hear him from the other side of the store. It gave me anxiety since we didn't know if there was something with us, but they'd know we were there. In one aisle I chose to go down, there was a small packet of candy lying on the ground and I felt my heart jump with joy. It was a Better Bar, which wasn't the best candy, but it was candy nonetheless. I'd found something useful and I wasn't dead. I was satisfied with that, and even started to let my guard down. Aisle after aisle, I kept searching and picking up everything I could get my hands on. By the time I reached the back of the store, I had my Better Bar, a few cans of fruits and vegetables, and a small bag of carrots, which were slightly questionable but seemed mostly edible.

By the time I started heading toward the clothing section, I couldn't hear Donnie anymore. I poked my head out and looked toward the entrance, but he was nowhere to be found. Finally, he'd remembered how to search quietly. When I reached the clothes, everything we could use was gone. Some kid's clothes and pants, which were torn so badly they wouldn't offer much more coverage than a single paper towel, were all that was left.

I decided that this section was a waste of time and turned to leave, but something caught my eye. The beam from my flashlight bounced off something in the distance. As I got closer, the stench of rust began wafting in the air. I soon remembered the smell and knew it was blood. I popped my knife open and cautiously approached. With each step, the shining object began to take shape, and what it was attached to. It was an arm with a golden watch wrapped around it, poking out from behind an old bin of ragged clothes. The arm belonged to the corpse of an old man. He was face down, but I could tell he was at least sixty, and there was blood pooling around his head. The body looked as if it had just died; he'd only been there for a few hours at the most. There weren't any marks or cuts that should've killed him. He'd just dropped dead.

I decided it was time to leave, but turning around was the worst mistake I could've made. A Creep was standing a few feet away from me. It was massive like a giant, practically scraping its head against heaven's door. Lifeless eyes had rolled to the back of its skull, and a thick tar came from its mouth to cover the body in a throbbing web. The way its head was cocked to the side made it look like a curious dog. I slowly moved away until I felt a dull pain on the side of my thigh, and I realized it was my pocket knife reminding me that it was still there. There was nothing I could think of doing besides plunging the blade directly into its stomach, so that's exactly what I did. It slid in like butter, but when I tried pulling it out again, it was like trying to pull it from solid cement. I had no choice but to leave my weapon stuck where it was. The creature didn't seem affected, as it reached a hand towards me, causing me to stumble foolishly over my own feet. I started to crawl away and ended up touching something warm. I lifted my hand: it was the blood of the old man, now dripping down my arm. Thinking I'd need to climb over the corpse to keep fleeing, I turned to see where I needed to go, but the man wasn't lying there anymore. In fear, I watched as the old man stood back up, and his mouth was torn open by a dark, slug-like creature that emerged out of his throat.

Couldn't go forward, and couldn't go back. I was stuck between death and the grave. I hoped that crossing my arms in front of my face would lessen the blow somehow. Praying that it wouldn't be as bad as it seemed, I gave up and waited.

There was the sound of stomping feet, then five loud pops flying towards me. I turned to see Donnie standing at the other end of the aisle, smoke billowing from his gun. The old man was back on the floor but now had blood pooling from bullet holes. Donnie lifted his gun and shot the Creep just as it was going to touch my face. When it fell to the floor, he stood over it and unloaded the rest of his gun into the creature. It writhed in what seemed like pain, before the black tar turned to vapers, leaving behind the mangled mess of a human.

"Let's go!" he screamed as he picked me up over his shoulder.

He carried me outside, placed me down, and we continued to run from the Pukes and Creeps flooding from the Super Shop. We must've run a mile before Donnie said it was okay to stop. He threw his bag on the ground and put his hands on top of his head.

"I told you not to go in there!" he yelled. "You have to listen to me... Dammit!"

I wanted to tell him that he was wrong, but he was so mad at me. I knew it was my fault somehow. There was nothing I could do or say, just stand there. I'd fucked up again, and Donnie had to sort it all out. I wanted to apologize but I couldn't. I was sick of saying sorry, and if saying it was old to me, I knew hearing it was ancient to him. In that moment, I truly wished for something to end me and the burden I put on others.

I placed my bag on the ground and took out the food from the store. He ripped it all from my hands and began to study it. Staring at me, he tore open the bag of carrots and dumped them on the ground.

"What did you leave behind?" he questioned.

"...I forgot..."

Donnie cursed and threw the Better Bar back in the direction of the Super Shop. His head snapped toward me and his expression filled me with fear. His eyes were vibrant red and he was breathing like a wild animal.

"Did you know of any other exits?" he growled.

I still didn't have any words to say to him. I could hardly look at him. I folded my arms and shook my head. He laughed in a sort of pissed-off way, then he scooped up his bag, threw it on his shoulders and continued down the road. We walked for an hour or two without saying a single word. I hated the silence, so I decided to break it and ask where he was from. I figured it was a good question to ask and one I was surprised I hadn't thought of earlier. He grunted that he was from here. I felt my face twist from the awkwardness. I elaborated on the question since I meant where he was from before all this started. Donnie's eyes snapped onto me and I winced, thinking he'd yell again, but he didn't. He took a few deep breaths, rubbed his head and told me there were some cars in the distance he wanted to look in.

Donnie made a beeline towards them, so I followed behind. All of the cars were either smashed to bits or stripped down to nothing, but that didn't stop us from looking. We searched some of them, but anything useful had already been taken. Some houses lined the street next to us, but they were all either boarded up or burnt to a crisp. I looked toward Donnie, but his eyes were fixed on something else. I followed the path of his stare and saw a pristine motorcycle sitting in the middle of all the cars.

Donnie ran up and began inspecting it, but it gave me a rotten feeling. The motorcycle was a beautiful charcoal color, and had handle bars that stretched high into the sky. It didn't seem like something that someone would just leave out in the open, but it was nice to see Donnie smile again. He had been so mad for most of the day, but now he was grinning ear to ear. I started jogging up next to him when I heard a metal click.

"Let's not make any type of movement, y'all hear?" a voice shouted from behind a car.

Three men stood and pointed guns at us. Donnie lowered his

hand and placed it on his pistol. One of the men yelled for him to take it easy and no one would be hurt. I looked back at Donnie and he was looking at me. He closed his eyes, then slowly put his hands into the air. I followed his lead.

The trio came over to us, patted down our pockets and looked through our bags. Everything that could have been used as a weapon was taken. The man who had been talking to us introduced himself as Kevin. His hair was tied back in an oily ponytail, and every piece of his clothing was camouflage, even his boots. The others were introduced as Ralph and Monty. Those two looked pretty much the same, with their bald heads and flavor saver beards, except that Ralph had milky white skin and Monty was dark as midnight.

Kevin instructed us to follow them, but I was frozen stiff, not knowing if we were just going to listen or try and fight. When I looked at Donnie, he was staring wide-eyed at the ground, and that told me we were doing what they asked. There was no time to think or stall because Monty and Ralph pressed their guns into our heads and shoved us forward.

The walk was silent. Whenever I tried whispering to Donnie, I was told to shut up. Once, I didn't hear the demand to be quiet, but before I could finish saying Donnie's name, I was clubbed on the back of the head. My body tumbled to the ground before my mind knew what was happening. Ralph was standing over me, a gun pointed at my head. He went to open his mouth to say something, but Donnie tackled him to the ground, sending his gun flying over to me. I picked it up and aimed it just as Ralph started beating Donnie. I yelled for him to stop, but the cowardice shake in my voice rang out. I took a breath, knowing I could kill this man, but just as I placed my finger on the trigger, a shot rang out behind me.

"Now enough of this bullshit!" Kevin hollered. "Ralph, get your ass up and that gun back in your damn hand!"

Donnie demanded I shoot him dead, but I couldn't. Kevin told me that if Ralph died, Donnie died with him. Ralph walked over and grabbed me. Donnie screamed for him to get away from me and went to jump to his feet, but Ralph spun around and pointed the gun at his head. I saw Donnie's body tense as he went to make a move for Ralph again, but Kevin hollered out that I may get hurt in the scuffle. Donnie looked at me, growled and relaxed his body.

"See, that wasn't bad, now, was it?" he asked, looking at me and smiling.

I stared up at him, emotionless. He yelled at Ralph for hitting me and said that he could see some potential in us already. He walked me back to Donnie and told Ralph and Monty not to touch me like that again, or he'd make sure they were paid back.

The rest of that day, and into the night, was spent walking down the jagged and beaten road. The weather turned to freezing and caused my body to cramp. Kevin said we were almost there, which I felt a sense of undeserving relief for. My body was rattled with stress and I couldn't feel my feet. We reached the top of a grassy hill, and Kevin, pointing towards the horizon, exclaimed that we were home. It was a massive building made of white brick. The base wasn't very impressive in length, but there was a center portion that jetted up into the sky.

As we got closer, I saw the word *Mall* plastered along a dilapidated sign. This was a place I definitely would've known about before the downfall, but I had no clue. Thinking back, I didn't recognize anywhere we had been. In that moment, I realized how far away from home I'd gotten and how alone that made me feel. I was a helpless idiot, along for the ride as long as

I could take before dropping dead.

The parking lot was riddled with forgotten cars, and an army-green gate that surrounded the mall. There was a woman standing behind the gate who had a gun trained on us. As we approached the building, Kevin gave her a wave. She dropped her gun and let us in. Kevin had some words with her, and when she looked at me, I looked down at the floor. I could feel her eyes piercing my body like a nail being driven through wood. The urge to run or try to fight crossed my mind a few times as we walked, but it wasn't strong enough to make me act. Before I could formulate any type of plan to get myself and Donnie away, we were being pulled inside.

I closed my eyes until my feet began squeaking on a silky floor. When I scanned the area, I saw a few people standing around and talking to each other as if nothing was wrong in the world. The dirty black floors were offset by the pearlescent white walls and the four pillars that stood in the middle of the space. It seemed like a normal day at a mall, just with many fewer people in the stores that lined the hall. All of these people were acting like nothing was going on outside. They were just like the people with Georgie. They were liars to each other and liars to themselves. It made my skin crawl.

At the end of the long hallway, there was a small store. Our three escorts put us inside and brought down a cage, shutting off the store from the rest of the mall. After we were confined, they left us, but not before saying that they hoped we enjoyed our stay.

Donnie let out a sigh and slumped down onto the floor. I asked what we were going to do and he told me to let him think, but that wasn't a good enough answer for me. I felt like my body was miles underwater, trying to swim with a weighted vest. I had no idea who these people were, if they knew the people from the convenient store, or what they wanted with us. I ran to each corner of the room to look for some sort of exit. There was a small vent on the ceiling, but it was too high to reach and filled with white foam.

"Funny how lessons come back to people when there is no point for them," Donnie said, chuckling to himself.

Even if he was right, I had to keep searching. Maybe there would be something like a tool they'd forgotten about, something sharp, or a crack in the foundation. I thought there had to be something in that room that we could use to get out, but again, Donnie was right. There was nothing. Everything was picked clean besides the counter, which was bolted to the floor. Panicked, I huddled behind it. Georgie's yellow teeth glowed in my memory and it made my body ache. Donnie called out to me just as I was about to fall into my head. He asked me to stand and look at him, so I did, trying not to let my panic show.

"Easy times make shit survivors... We will not let our circumstances define us as fearful and weak. We are brave and we are strong, no matter what we deal with," he said with a smile, but it wasn't the genuine one he'd normally give. This one looked forced and nervous.

He went back to sitting in the corner of the room and staring at the people outside. I returned to my place and thought about myself. I was a survivor, a scavenger, and a killer. Even when I wasn't sure if I wanted to anymore, I still sucked air into my lungs. That had to account for something. I had to let that something take over and allow me to be brave – or at least make it show as much as I could force it to.

We both sat in the store for what seemed like days. Finally, footsteps started coming towards us. It was Kevin, with the woman from the front gate right behind him. Donnie smiled at me, then stood to meet them at the cage, and I hopped up and stood at his side. Donnie and I didn't say a word as Kevin approached us with a cheery 'hello.' He tried small talk, like asking if we liked the mall, if we were treated okay, and if we needed anything. The only thing Donnie growled in response was, "Let us out."

"Well, unfortunately, we can't do that for ya, buddy," Kevin replied. "We don't know who the hell y'all even are."

Kevin continued to tell us about what was going to take place. He said that we'd spend the night in the store, then in the morning there would be an opportunity for us to work for them. Donnie didn't look amused by what he had to say.

"Call it an even trade," Kevin continued. "We let y'all sleep here, in safety. Y'all do something for us in return." He told us to have a goodnight, then turned his back and walked away. The woman who was with him looked at me with that piercing glare, then followed Kevin.

Donnie was still standing motionless behind the bars, but I noticed that his hands, held behind his back, were trembling like leaves caught in a storm. He balled them into fists and said we were going to get out of there.

We sat together, watching people walk past. They all seemed like they didn't know what was happening outside. Like time had stopped ticking for them when the Pukes came. Their act made me tired. I laid my body down on the gritty floor in a halfhearted attempt at sleep. After some time, Donnie nudged me to let me know that Kevin was coming back. We sprung to our feet and took the same position we had before.

"Didn't mean to disturb," Kevin said as he reached the cage, "I'm just here with… well, let's call it a peace offering." There was a large cut out in the cage that Kevin used to slide in a bottle of whiskey and a slice of chocolate cake. "Saw you had some in your bag, so I thought it'd be nice to give y'all a better one. And who the hell wouldn't want some cake?"

Kevin waited for one of us to take it, but I knew I wasn't going to move. I knew we were going to stare him down, make him feel uncomfortable, then at our first opportunity, ditch this place. Donnie asked where he'd gotten the booze, and Kevin told him that they'd found an abandoned liquor store a few miles down that was stocked to the brim. "Needing alcohol now more than ever," Kevin said with a slight giggle.

We waited like statues till Kevin turned his back, leaving the things with us. I sat on the floor, but Donnie stayed at the gate. My stomach grumbled at the sight of the cake and the way the frosting glistened in the dim moonlight, but I knew I couldn't have it. I was strong and knew that when we got out, we'd find food worth waiting for. That confidence changed when Donnie bent over to scoop up the bottle of booze. He said it would be a shame to let that go to waste. He explained he still felt sick from drinking the night before and a few sips would help take the edge off. I thought we were supposed to be fearless, and act cold-hearted towards them until they let us go, but clearly something had changed. Donnie opened the bottle quickly like a child on Christmas morning and chugged it. Watching him pour the liquid down his throat made me uneasy. Why did he need to do that now?

"We show them we're fearful, they own our souls," he whispered. "You have to be strong. It isn't a question of whether you can, because you have no choice." After speaking, he slumped against the wall. He asked if I would split the cake with him, so that's what we did.

It didn't make sense to me. Why would he flip so easily? My

feelings of uncertainty and confusion continued to grow the more I thought about it. In what seemed like seconds, the shine of the sun replaced the moon's light. It was nice to know I'd been kept alive through the night, but I quickly thought that would change. Thudding steps marched down the long hall. The lady from the front gate was coming towards us. She was a black woman with beautifully poufy, chestnut-colored hair. Aggravation scrolled out across her face, and the blood stains on her clothes told me to be careful around her.

"You," she said, pointing to me. "You're coming with me."

She flung open the cage and headed towards me. I turned to Donnie, but he was still passed out on the floor. I tried waking him but he answered only with grumbles. His scent was a mix of putrid bowels, tared teeth, and a belly full of booze. Clearly, Donnie wasn't going to be able to help, so I needed to take care of this myself. She pulled me out and closed the cage behind us. She let go of my arm and told me to follow her. Those feelings of nothingness, emptiness, sadness, and bitterness all began festering in the pit of my stomach as I followed her down the hall.

"Name's Rebeca," she snapped. A couple of seconds passed before she looked down at me. "And you are…?"

"Alexandria," I said plainly.

We continued walking and she asked me the occasional question, like where I was from, how old I was, and how long I'd been with Donnie. I refused to give her extra information on us so I kept my responses as quick and as punctual as possible. Truly, I was too focused on not letting her see my knees tremble with every step I took to pay any real attention to what she said.

We walked down the main hall for a bit, and I could tell that they were using each store for something different. The one we were locked in was clearly the jail, but some along the hall seemed to be for housing. One kept all the medical supplies and had a few lily-white beds in it.

There was a sound like a boiling teapot screaming in the distance. We kept getting closer to the sound until I recognized what it was: a baby's cry. Once we reached the store where the cry was coming from, I saw a fussing baby cradled in a woman's arms. It couldn't have been more than a few weeks old. There was another child playing on the floor, and they didn't seem more than just a few months old. This store was filled with color, toys and pictures, with vibrant paint slapped on all of the walls. The woman holding the baby looked up and smiled at me. The urge to smile was strong, but I was able to crush it. I couldn't deny that it was so amazing to see new life in this old, dying world, though. I looked at Rebeca, who was staring down at me.

"Thought they were all dead?"

The whole sight felt almost hopeful, like a kept promise that life will continue through this mess. But that hope proved fleeting when I thought of these kids being forced to live in the new world and the inevitability of their deaths, probably sooner rather than later. Before I could get comfortable in my thoughts, Rebeca gripped my shoulder and pulled me back down the hallway.

"You can visit the daycare later… maybe," she said.

She escorted me outside and to the first place I'd laid eyes on her: the gate. Getting a closer look at it, I could see the stains of blood and coal-colored slime mixing well with the deeply etched scratches.

"I don't know what's happening with you yet, but what I do know is that you'll be helping with things as long as you're here," Rebeca said as she pulled a gun from her side and thudded it down on a metal table next to her. Then she pulled out a large jug filled with water and a rag. "Clean," she instructed, pointing towards the gate.

The blast of cold made my arms sore as I grabbed the nasty jug and the stringy rag. My hands trembled as I picked pieces of flesh and decay off the gate. I spent hours cleaning, and Rebeca spent those hours watching me. Not a word was said until she broke the silence.

"I'll ask you again," she barked. "You know that man?"

I didn't say a word, just nodded that I did know him.

"How long?" she questioned.

I felt like a degenerate cleaning that gate, so my way of getting her back was to be silent. Or maybe I was afraid of saying the wrong thing. Either way, I knew she wasn't getting information out of me.

"Clearly, both of you would like to stay here till the winter months end… correct?" she asked.

I thought staying quiet had been the best course of action, but that seemed questionable when she told me to follow her. We walked back inside the mall, but then Rebeca pulled me down a hall I hadn't noticed before. It was dark as coal and the only light was coming from a tiny sliver peeking out from under a door at the very end.

I was going to die in that room, but in its own way, that was funny to me. Donnie had told me we would be tough, cold, and give them nothing; that would keep us safe. Ironically, he was the one safe in the store, drunk off a gifted drink, while I'd done what he'd asked, and I was going to die from it. The thought of turning to Rebeca and telling her my life story did cross my mind, but I couldn't. Maybe out of the miniscule amount of pride I still had left, maybe because Donnie told me not to, or maybe the biggest reason I stayed quiet was because this could have been a way out of this horrible world. The one who I'd thought would be with me and help me was in a drunken stupor, not even aware that I had left. I just wanted to see my family again. I was pretty positive I couldn't make myself go and see them, but these people would. That was enough for me to keep quiet and see how it played out. Besides, I preferred the idea of being a silent badass as the bullet tore through my skull, instead of a talkative ass trying to save a life worth nothing.

As we got to the door and Rebeca grasped the handle, I heard a terrible scream, the type that makes glass shatter and milk curdle. It sounded just like my mother's scream. My knees kept giving out under the weight of my body. I knew Rebeca could see it. She twisted the doorknob and flung open the pale green door.

CHAPTER 7

There was silence as I waited with bated breath for my body to hit the floor. When nothing happened for longer than I thought necessary for a fall, I opened my eyes and saw something I'd never thought I would again: a rock wall. It stretched so far into the air that I could hardly see the top. I began laughing loudly at the sight of my death room. They were going to kill me in front of a fucking rock wall. I used to have a mini one attached to my outdoor playset, and I loved it. Now I'd die at the foot of one. It was almost amusing.

"We ain't gonna hurt ya, kid," Kevin chimed in as he stepped towards me. "No need to be uptight."

A man who I didn't recognize stood towards the back of the group. He was staring down at his own frantic hand movements, not saying a word. Kevin placed his hand on the man's back and gave him a nudge towards me. He sheepishly looked through his brow and came closer.

"I'm Lesley," he said as he stuck out his hand, "but people normally call me Les."

I wasn't sure how to respond, so I gripped his hand as tightly as I could and shook it. "Alexandria... Alex," I said.

He clutched his hand to his chest and stretched out his fingers. Maybe I'd gone a bit overboard with how hard I'd gripped or maybe he was weak. Kevin said that Les needed to tell me something, so I stared at him and waited for whatever he wanted to share.

"Do you know Donnie?" he asked.

At that point, I was pretty sick of hearing that same question from different people. I quickly answered that I did know him and we'd been together for a few weeks.

"I knew it wasn't her," he muttered under his breath as his face grew pale and his eyes went back to the floor. "I used to know Donnie... before all this. He... he isn't someone good."

This guy, Les, talking about Donnie started to piss me off. How could he speak about someone and say they were bad, despite probably not truly knowing them? So I didn't take what he said too seriously and brushed off his comment with a shrug.

"He drinks around you, doesn't he?" Les asked, and I nodded carelessly. "When he drinks, he doesn't stop till he's out, right?" he continued. Again, I nodded, but tried to hide the fact I was listening to his words carefully now.

I asked why that mattered, pointing out that tons of people drank but that didn't mean they were bad. He told me I was right, but that Donnie became different when he drank. I figured I should speak up to defend Donnie.

"None of you know a thing about Donnie. He is my friend and he's saved my life more times than I can count. If he likes to drink after all we've been through, that's fine."

The three of them turned away from me and began to talk with each other. As I waited for them to finish their pow-wow, I looked up at the massive rock wall. At the very top, there was a small space to stand and a hatch that seemed to lead to the roof. A man was climbing the wall with something strapped to his chest. It wasn't a harness for safety. It looked more like the type of pack used to carry a child.

"Okay," Kevin said, "ya can stay... for now, at least."

I looked at them with a baffled expression, and said that we had no intention of staying.

"Well, it seems like you don't have much choice in the matter, considering present circumstances..." He pointed to a window, showing the small flurries of snow starting to fall.

They told me that we could either stay there with them and see how things panned out, or we could go back outside and freeze in the next few weeks. I had no idea what to do. If we stayed, we could die at their hands. If we left, we could freeze. There was one question in the back of my mind that really bothered me: why were they being so disgustingly nice to us? I mean, they had no reason to be kind, and the fact that they were put my mind on edge.

"What do you get out of us staying?" I asked.

"Work," Rebeca said without hesitation.

Kevin gave her a few pats on the shoulder, then moved her to the side. "See, what she meant to tell ya, in a much kinder way, is that we can't maintain this place without work being done. Simple as that, kid."

The excuse made sense, but it was still just words, not action. I told them that Donnie and I would stay for now, just so they'd drop the subject. Once I got back to Donnie, we'd think of what we should do.

"If you both plan on staying, there is one thing you need to know," Les chimed in, "Donnie hurt people... He hurt people before all this happened. And he especially did when he drank." Les said that as long as Donnie was kept in check, we both could stay. If not, Donnie would need to go.

"Don't be so overdramatic." Kevin chastised Les. "A drink ain't gonna kill nobody."

Les just closed his eyes and shook his head.

"Welp, it's settled," Kevin said in a celebratory voice. "Let's celebrate with a drink!" His joke didn't seem to amuse anyone but himself.

"You'll learn how our system works in the morning," Rebeca said. "For now, I'm taking you back to your room."

When we got back to the jail, Donnie was standing at the cage, clutching the metal bars with white knuckles. As Rebeca slid open the cage for me to crawl under, Donnie grabbed for her ankles. She pulled the cage down onto his arms, making him scream in pain before calling her a horrid bitch. Rebeca laughed about it and said she would see us in the morning. Donnie's lips pursed like a viper ready to strike. I called out to him and put my finger to my lips. He locked his eyes on me before letting out an exhale that made his body sink. He didn't say a word and watched Rebeca leave.

"What the hell happened? Where did they take you? Did they hurt you?" Donnie asked quickly. "I swear, if they touched you, I'll kill every person who breathes in this whole place!"

He rushed back to the cage, even though I tried stopping him, and repeated that everyone would die if we weren't released. Just as he finished his verbal tirade, Lesley could be seen walking down the hall, staring at him. Donnie widened his eyes and sat back down on the floor without saying another word.

"That guy there," Donnie said just a touch louder than a whisper, "he talked to you?"

"Yeah... seems like a weird dude. He says he knew you," I answered while Donnie looked down at the bruising on his hands.

"Yeah, we know each other," he continued. "I, um... me and his wife had an affair."

Now it made a bit more sense as to why Les didn't like Donnie. He'd said that Donnie was a bad guy who hurt people because Donnie had hurt him. It was a disgusting thing to do, to try and make me hate him off lies, but I understood.

"Just don't talk to him, okay? He... he just starts trouble for me," Donnie said. I told him I'd keep to myself around him. Donnie seemed pretty happy with that idea.

I sat next to him and started looking at his hands. Thankfully, they weren't broken, just extra banged up. Then a slightly sweet, woody smell started wafting. I recognized it as alcohol. Even though I knew he was a liar, Les' words of warning rang in my head.

"You think you can hold off on the drinking tonight?" I asked, trying not to sound like I'd gotten the idea from anyone but myself.

His face grew a confused expression. "Of course I can... What makes you ask that?"

"I just think it would do you– us some good if your senses were sharp," I answered, still not sure how he'd react.

"I need you to understand something, Alex," he started, with a tone that sounded secretive. "I don't need to drink at all. But it's something that helps... keep me calm. Believe me, you and everyone else in here needs me calm right now, so just a few drinks shouldn't worry your little head."

He sounded irritated by the question, which made me feel bad for doubting him, so I smiled and let it go. He gave me a pat on the shoulder, then reached back, grabbed the alcohol, and finished off what little liquid was left in the bottle.

We both said our goodnights, then faced away from each other. I thought about how silly it was for me to ask Donnie to stop drinking. I mean, he was right, after all. He hadn't been drinking all the time we were together, and whenever he did find alcohol, he'd wait till we were safe to drink it.

I tried to close my eyes, but my mind was playing a random

image game with me. At first it would be Georgie standing over me, then my parents blaming me for their death, then it was the man I'd shot turning and calling me a killer. After a while of trying, I gave up on the idea of any restful sleep and started studying the room. It seemed like Donnie was having the same problem, as he tossed, turned, cursed, then sat up and stared out into the mall.

Before the sun began to shine, marching rang out from down the hall. It was Rebeca coming towards us, and Donnie was already standing. I didn't want another smashed hand or something worse to happen, so I sprung to my feet and stood with him.

"You," she said to Donnie. "You're with Kevin. He'll be here in a few to collect you." Then she turned her gaze on me. "You're with me again, so let's go."

She slid open the cage far enough that I could duck underneath, but before I could, Donnie grabbed me. He leaned in and told me to get as much information as I could. A smell like wet dog covered his body, and the stench of dried alcohol wafted from his mouth. I gave him a nod and headed out. He didn't seem very happy about me leaving, but what other option was there?

"If anything happens to her," he said as he stood and addressed Rebeca again, "I'll slit your throat."

"Hands need to heal first," Rebeca replied with a grin.

Donnie's face twisted as he began bringing his hand up from his side, but I stopped him by saying that I'd be fine. Rebeca slammed the cage down just after I ducked under, almost closing it on my heels. She smiled at Donnie, but he was expressionless. He turned his back on us and sat back down.

Rebeca and I walked down the hall towards the front door in silence until she snapped at me, "You and your guy need to get something straight; neither of you are the boss around here." I told her I understood, but she firmly continued with her point. "No, you don't. Maybe no one filled you in on how it works around here, but Les, Kevin and I, we say what is or isn't. You two don't like that, leave. I don't give a fuck if you freeze."

I didn't know what to say in response, so I just kept quiet and kept walking. The numbingly cold air hit my skin like a truck when she opened the door and we stepped outside. At least the feeling of awkwardness that flooded my body was slightly relieved when I noticed there was a person already out there. It was the same woman who I'd seen watching the kids the day before. She turned around and greeted us with a hearty 'good morning.' Rebeca muttered one in response, and I just smiled.

Rebeca threw the jug of water and rag at my feet, then directed me to keep cleaning the gate. The woman said how silly it was for me to be cleaning since it was just going to get that way again. Her voice was so sweet sounding, which made for a nice change of pace.

"That IS the whole point," Rebeca barked. "We need to keep this gate strong and clean, so if there is another threat that pushes up on it, it won't fold like tissue."

"Well, at least give her a coat for being out here," the woman said.

Rebeca replied that they didn't have extra. The woman took off her coat and draped it over me. She instructed me to keep it as long as I needed since she had others. For the first time since being brought there, I made sure to show gratitude and thanked her with a smile. Her name was Erica. She had a very pretty face, but a body that was shaped like an egg yolk, which wasn't helped by her pink floral shirt and vibrant green pants. Her looks weren't the first thing I noticed though; it was how positive she seemed to be. She mentioned that she and her husband, Peter, had two babies named Jillian and Anthony. Either she or Peter were always watching the kids while the other was sleeping or out front. Rebeca stopped her from talking to me, and told her to go in and rest. We smiled at each other before she headed inside.

The gate was disgusting, especially now that everything was extra hard from the cold, so I had to pick off every particle of mold and flesh with my fingers. That's what I did for hours, while Rebeca sat on a small lawn chair. It really irritated me, but I couldn't muster up what to say about it. It was one thing for me to act tough, but inside, I was still quivering with fear about being alone with these people.

All of a sudden, Rebeca stood and told me to stop moving. Her rifle was aimed at something out in the parking lot. I didn't see anything at all, but I did hear it: the gentle sound of crying. It was almost like the sound of a disciplined child trying not to let their parents hear them as they wept.

The more I studied the lot, the more noise I was able to pick up. From behind one of the old cars that had been left behind, a Creep stepped out. Rebeca pointed her gun at it, but before she pulled the trigger, a Puke stepped out from one of the cars, then another, then another, and before we knew it, there were five Pukes marching towards us. Each of them screamed in pain as they were forced to come closer to the gate. With our attention on them, the Creep disappeared.

I started frantically searching for the Creep, but Rebeca yelled for me to focus on what was in front of me. She told me to keep watch on the corners so none of them could get past. A group was gathering on Rebeca's side, and she began firing at them. The sight of the Pukes terrified and angered me, and before I knew it, my back was pressed up against the far side of the gate.

My ears rang, and my vision tunneled on each of the Pukes as their bodies exploded from the bullets tearing through them. I closed my eyes and focused on my breathing, knowing that if I wanted to help, I needed to be calm. When my eyes opened up again, I was ready, willing and able to fight back.

I took a step towards Rebeca, then another. It was going to be easy; there weren't many of them, and we had the protection of the gate. Just as I took my third step, there was a large thud behind me. When I turned, I found the Creep, or rather, it found me and joined us on the inside of the gate.

I wasn't sure if the black creature could feel excitement, but it definitely seemed that way by how it vibrated along its host's skin. It reached both arms towards me and I froze in place. Thank God my knees lost their will to support me, because they gave way just before the monster touched me. My body flopped to the floor and snapped me from my frozen trance. I screamed for Rebeca to throw me something to kill it with, but instead, she started loading bullets into the Creep. Just as it seemed to be dying, the gun jammed. The Creep started running towards me.

Knowing I had to do something, I crawled back to Rebeca's lawn chair and threw it. Obviously, that didn't do anything close to killing it, but it did cause the monster to lose balance and stumble back a few steps. Finally, another shot rang out from Rebeca's gun. The bullet struck the Creep's shoulder, spinning it like a top. I heard Rebeca putting another round in the chamber, but there was no way she would have it ready in time. The Creep started to race towards me again. I threw my arms up in a weak attempt to stop it, but the front door did that for me.

It flung open and a wall of bullets came from inside, striking the Creep all over its body, and causing it to collapse. Les, Kenny and Donnie rushed out from inside with guns drawn. When

Donnie saw me on the ground, he knelt at my side and started checking me over, asking if I was hurt. I told him I was fine and watched as the human portion of the Creep writhed on the floor like it was possessed. The black substance slipped from the body and formed a puddle before turning to vapor. Before I could see any more, Donnie pulled me inside. He kept asking where I was hurt, and when I told him I was fine, it was like he was deaf, or I was mute.

Les came in, followed by Kevin and Rebeca. Those two headed to the medical store, but Les came towards me. Donnie coiled as Les started asking if I was okay. Donnie barked that I was fine and would be perfect if he wasn't around me. I called out to Donnie and told him that he needed to stop yelling. He didn't even look at me when I spoke, just marched over to me, grabbed my arm, and walked me back to the store we'd been held in.

"What was that all about?" I asked since it seemed odd that Donnie was so mad.

"You don't need to be talking to him. He is a thief. Nothing coming from him is anything good," he replied.

I thought that Donnie was the technical 'thief,' which made him the 'bad person.' When I took a breath to ask that, Donnie looked at me, veins popping from his neck, so I figured it would be best to just let it go. Just as my body began shaking from the withheld nerves, a voice rang out from behind us.

"She's fine!" Donnie snapped at the person.

"Oh, I know she is. I made sure of it." The voice was Rebeca's. She now had a few bandages around her arms and legs. "At least you didn't cower like I thought you would, though. So… good job, I guess."

Donnie seemed to be getting more pissed off with every

word spoken to him. The muscles in his jaw clamped down as his lips separated like a ravenous wolf. Before he could speak, Rebeca said that they made up beds for us to stay in. Donnie's face changed from one of pure rage, to one of confusion.

"Stay…?" he asked.

"I guess no one told you, but both of you are welcome to stay here through the winter," Rebeca explained, but her tone was patronizing.

Donnie started to ask what made them think that we'd stay with them for any longer than we were forced to. Rebeca answered that no one was forcing us to stay, but it would be the smart thing to do. She also mentioned to him that I'd agreed to stay. He didn't say another word, just rubbed his brow and followed Rebeca as she led us to our new store.

There were two sets of bunk beds, and one had our bags on them. I ran over to look inside and saw that everything was still in my bag, except my knife. I pulled out the Amy doll and looked it over. The dirty, broken expression on its face put a smile on mine. I was so accustomed to sleeping on concrete or hardwood floors that the new bed felt like I was laying on clouds. I hardly noticed the occasional bug that crawled across. The pillow and blanket looked like they were stuffed tablecloths, but I didn't care; it was amazing. I looked up at Donnie, who was still standing next to Rebeca. He looked disgusted, like I was sitting in putrid garbage.

"You're soft," he said. When I went up to him and asked what he meant, he said, "You just took this offer from these people that we hardly know. You put us in danger." He said he needed to take a walk to clear his head, then he left the room. I was going to go with him but he told me not to follow him. It took me off guard. I knew he'd be upset, but I definitely didn't expect a reaction like that.

Rebeca told me about the cafeteria and invited me to go with her, but I wanted to look around at my new living space. There was no other exit from the store except the entrance into it. The first thing that I wanted to try on the bed was sleep. Just as I began to doze, there was a bang that made my eyes fly open like curtains.

Georgie was walking down the basement steps. I reached to my sides and felt a rock that I wanted to use to smash him on his head, but when I tried lifting it, it felt like it weighed ten thousand pounds and wouldn't budge. I tried to stand and run, but my leg was chained to the foot of the bed. I started begging him to leave me alone, but he just kept getting closer. He pulled a knife from his pocket and told me that Donnie wasn't coming, then stabbed the blade into my side.

CHAPTER 8

My body was flung forward, and I realized I was still in my bunk bed, but there was a very real poking at my side. It was from a girl that seemed to be around my age.

"Well, good morning, sleepy," she said with pep in her voice.

When I tried responding, it was like I was choking on air. My body was so tense that I couldn't move. Having no clue what to say or do in response, I just smiled. It must've been an awkward or weird smile because this girl laughed in my face when I did. Then an unfamiliar male voice echoed from the back of the store.

"That's enough, Chelsea," the man's voice instructed. "She doesn't need you annoyin' her." After the person finished speaking, he walked around to the foot of my bed and introduced himself. "Hello, I'm Tommy and you've already met Chelsea," he said.

Chelsea waved at me aggressively, then said how nice it was to meet me. Tommy stuck out his hand and I shook it. Then he pulled Chelsea off the bed as she shouted that we would hang out later.

I peeked over the edge and saw that they slept on the bunk beds across from ours. Even though Chelsea seemed high-strung, I thought it might be nice to have someone around my age to talk to. Maybe she could even be a friend. That made me start thinking about Donnie and where he was. The sun was starting to set, so he had been gone for much longer than a walk should have taken. I didn't mind leaving the bed, since it now made me feel dirty. I hopped out and went to find him.

The woman I'd met earlier in the day, Erica, was talking to someone. When I walked over to them, Erica stopped her conversation and gave me a big hug before asking if I was okay. I told her I was fine, just a bit shaken up. She nodded her head like she understood.

"Gosh, where are my manners? Alex, this is my husband, Peter."

He had a thin frame with an amazing beard that reached down to his shoulders. It was probably to make up for the lack of hair on his head. He stuck out his hand, and when I grabbed it to shake, he pulled me in for a hug. It seemed really odd, but also nice. When he said hello to me, after the hug, I noticed that his voice was just as jolly and promising as Erica's.

I asked if they'd seen the man who I'd been with, and they told me that he'd been walking up and down the halls for a long time, but that he'd stopped and gone into Kevin's room. They pointed it out to me and I headed straight there.

Just as I was about to turn into Kevin's room, he walked out and asked if I was joining the party. He chuckled then walked by me. When I entered the room, Donnie was standing and studying some pictures that were next to one of the beds. He looked back and smiled.

"Crazy, ain't it?" he asked. "They seem to have everything figured out... Perfection." His tone was full of a calm irritation. When I told him I'd like to stay here, at least for a while, he came and stood next to me. "Groups... they just aren't my thing, Alex," he said in a whisper. "But... that being said, I'm not going to leave your side."

He smiled as he finished, and I smiled back. He pulled me

into his chest and hugged me so tightly that I could hardly breathe. I was happy that he'd finally come to some sense and realized it was best to just stay here, even if it was just to stay with me. Unfortunately, that happiness was fleeting as I heard the sloshing of liquid behind me. I grabbed his arms and pulled them out in front of me. He was clutching a small bottle that claimed to be the world's best vodka on the label.

"Donnie… why do you have this?" I asked.

To think straighter, keep calmer, feel better, and function easier were some of the vague excuses he gave me. I asked him to do me a favor and to not drink for a few days. His head twisted to the side so hard that I thought his neck would crack.

"Stop drinking?" he asked. "If this place is so pristine and perfect, that means we are protected. That means I can drink and not worry. Sounds like true perfection to me. Besides, Kevin said I could help myself as long as I'd help him around here."

"What is it that you're trying to hide from?" I demanded as frustration built. "Every night you didn't drink, you'd stay awake all night, staring into the fire. Now that you have your drink, and know you can get it, you want to stay. What are you keeping secret?"

He went from irritated to angry in a heartbeat. He took a few steps back, then polished off the rest of the bottle. "We are here because of you, and you alone," he barked. "So, excuse me if I'm making the best out of this shitty situation."

He turned his back to me and opened a cabinet that was filled with booze. Again, he didn't answer me, just kept rummaging through the liquor. Feeling fed up with not being talked to, I went to grab his arm. He threw it backwards so aggressively that it knocked me off my feet.

"Damnit, I'm just going to have a little more, Car-!" He

yelled before falling silent.

He stood all the way up, but stared down at his shoes, the color draining from his face. I got to my feet and touched his hand, making his red eyes snap onto me, then slowly drift back down to the floor. He whispered that he was going to our store and left without saying another word. I followed at a distance until he reached our room. Tommy said hello, but there was no response, just the slight creek of the bed springs as Donnie climbed in. When I entered, Tommy was standing by Donnie's bed. I went up to him and said that his name was Donnie and he wasn't feeling too good.

Chelsea came over to me as I climbed up into my bunk. She started asking about stupid things like if I believed in unicorns, if I ever had a dog, and told me that her favorite animal was a bear. Honestly, the thought of telling her off did cross my mind a few times, but thankfully, Tommy came and pulled her away from me. He told her I'd had a long day and I needed to rest, and I couldn't have agreed more.

The mind is an interesting thing. My body was so exhausted that I felt like it would take all the strength in the world to move a single joint. But my thoughts were racing and felt as if they could keep going for years. Every time I'd let my eyes rest, instead of the feel of my bed under me, the concrete floor I was treated to with Georgie would press up against my bones. He'd be walking up to me, smiling like a devil and holding a bottle of alcohol in each hand. There was no way I'd be getting any sleep, and from the sound of it, neither would Donnie. He was throwing himself around like a wild bull. Eventually, he got up and began looking through his bag. I couldn't see him, but I could hear him. I listened for the booze, but never heard it. He was pretty vocal about how mad he was. I laid in my bunk until I heard footsteps marching down the hall, so I figured it was time to wake from my make-believe sleep. When my feet hit the floor, Donnie covered his ears, but did say good morning.

Rebeca strolled into the room with Kevin just behind her. By the time they came in, Donnie and I had already gotten up and put our packs on. They explained that Donnie would be with Kevin, and I'd be with Rebeca, the same as the day before. The only difference was that today, Donnie would be going out to scavenge with Kevin, Ralph and Monty. He didn't seem too happy about leaving me behind.

"You left her yesterday," Rebeca said, cleaning her rifle.

"Yes, but I was still here in the mall. You want me to just leave her behind completely."

I didn't want Donnie to leave, but not because I was scared about being alone in the mall. That feeling had subsided, mostly. I didn't want him leaving because I knew the type of thanks he'd get for his help.

Kevin looked at Donnie and said that he needed to work if he wanted to stay. Donnie sighed, then nodded that he understood. After he'd finished talking to Kevin, he came over to give me a hug, told me to be safe, then walked out into the hall.

Rebeca told Chelsea and Tommy that they were going with Les. Chelsea asked if I could go with them, but Rebeca said that she needed me for the day. Chelsea's face turned sour but I reassured her that we'd spend time together later.

"I'm going to teach you some new things today," Rebeca said as we left the room. "Have you ever used a gun before?"

"Once…"

"Good, so you can use one again."

She brought me into the room with the rock wall and we headed to the back corner. There was a door she needed to unlock, and behind it was a wall of rusty metal used to draw blood. On the wall hung at least six different types of long guns, like shotguns or rifles, a dozen handguns, and enough ammo to last a year. She showed me around, getting me semi-familiar with each one and their uses, which was pretty redundant. The biggest question to me was how and where they'd found so much ammo. She explained that they didn't find it, but made it. There was a large, square machine in the corner that had a big, brass handle on its side. She showed me how they collected empty bullet cases and different types of explosive powders and pressed the two together to make new bullets that were ready to use. The accuracy varied from bullet to bullet, depending on how well one had been made, but they would all fire.

Kevin said that he'd forgotten to get Donnie armed up as they joined us in the room. Rebeca told me to grab him a gun to use. When I looked in the cabinet to see what I could give him, I noticed Donnie's gun on the wall. I figured it would be better to be over equipped instead of under, so I handed him his gun and an all-black combat rifle. His face started glowing when I handed him his weapons. Just as quickly as the two men had entered the room, they left: Donnie gave me a hug, then Kevin said they'd be back before nightfall.

After they'd left, Rebeca explained that only she, Kevin and Les had a key to the weapons, and no one was allowed in without one of them knowing. That seemed counter-productive to me because if something were to happen to one, or all, of them, how would anyone be able to defend themselves? But I just kept my mouth shut.

Rebeca handed me a pistol and said I was going to use it today. As I was studying the weapon, a hand touched me on the shoulder. I jumped back and swung my arms wildly at whoever had touched me. It was Les, now doubled over in pain from my punch, which had hit him in the groin. I rushed to him to apologize, but he said that he understood.

"Next time, I'll just announce that I'm behind you, okay?" he squeaked out.

He went into the room and grabbed some weapons, then said goodbye to me and Rebeca. I asked what Les was doing and Rebeca said he was going to the garden. I was pretty sure things didn't grow in winter, but apparently I was wrong. It seemed odd that the gardeners would need weapons, but Rebeca told me that she and I were the first line of defense at the front of the mall, and with the garden placed out back, those people needed to be just as prepared to fight.

Once we got outside, Rebeca placed the weapons on the table and plopped down on one of the chairs. I stood by her, waiting for her to give me something to practice on with my gun, but all she did was look at me. Apparently, I still needed to finish cleaning the gate before I could learn anything about shooting.

For the next couple hours, I continued the monotonous job of scrubbing that disgusting gate. It added insult to injury when Rebeca went in and got herself a cup of water, but didn't offer me any. I just gritted my teeth and kept cleaning. The sun was at its full height when she finally told me I could take a break and sit in the chair next to her, so I did.

"Why don't you speak up when you want something?" she asked me as if I knew the answer. "I mean... I know you saw me with this water and I knew you would want some, but you didn't even ask... Why?"

I explained that my parents had always taught me to be polite, to be kind to others, even if they weren't nice back, and I guess it had just stuck. My answer made her laugh so hard she grabbed her stomach.

"You think being ladylike accounts for shit anymore?" she said when she stopped laughing in my face. I replied with a meek no. "Listen, you have a tough guy act going. But that will only get you so far when you still let people shit on you."

She explained that the world was now a hard place, harder than before. She said that now was the time to take what you wanted, and defend yourself without question. I knew she was right and I knew I had to make a change. I started with reaching out and grabbing the cup of water from Rebeca and drinking the last of it. She smiled and seemed satisfied that I was grasping the concept.

"So now," she said, "I'm going to teach you how to use this." She picked up the pistol from the table and handed it to me. She showed me how to check if it was loaded or empty and explained how to aim. She asked when I'd used a gun before.

"To kill a man," I said. "I didn't have to aim; I didn't have to practice. I just pointed the barrel to the back of his head and pulled the trigger."

She seemed surprised by the revelation that I was a murderer, but thankfully she didn't make me talk about it and moved on. My cleaning jug was still on the ground. She told me to aim and shoot a hole through the center. I locked my arms out in front of me and shot, missing by a mile. Rebeca told me to keep my arms loose to account for the recoil. I took aim again, and this time struck the ground right next to the jug. She told me how to adjust my aim and I did, so when I took my next shot, I pierced the center and threw it into the air.

"The most important thing for you to remember is that a gun is always loaded. Never point it at something you don't want destroyed," Rebeca said as she took the gun from my hands.

My face hurt from smiling, but then I heard a clattering. Quickly, I realized that it was coming from my teeth clicking together. My entire body began to tremble and my eyes watered so much I couldn't see straight. Panic started setting in, but as it did, I caught a glimpse of Rebeca watching me like I was walking a tightrope. I closed my eyes and took a breath, then another, and another until I was finally able to keep myself steady.

"Good," she said when I opened my eyes to look at her.

The sound of moaning was heading our way, but Rebeca didn't seem too worried. She told me that we were done with practice for the day. We waited around for the Pukes to show themselves, but they didn't seem to see us. Must've just come to check out the noise.

"Now, when it comes to them," Rebeca said, "just shoot for the chest and head. Kill the body, the creature inside dies too." I asked about the Creeps and how to kill them. "Same concept, but you need to be more precise with your shots. The black parts that cover the body seem to be bulletproof, so you need to strike the small parts of the human that peek through."

Some more time passed, and just before the sun set, Donnie and the scavenging group came over the horizon. As he got closer, I noticed his bag was filled to the point where a rip was a real possibility. Just as he passed through the gate, Donnie wrapped his arms around me and gave a tight squeeze. We all headed in together, and the scavenging group went to unload their findings. Just before he went to drop off everything in his bag, Donnie told me to go wait in our room because he didn't want me seeing the surprise that he'd got for me. It was a weird request, but I accepted.

My store was empty, which was nice. It meant I could relax and not have to maintain a conversation. Just as I was getting comfortable, Donnie strolled in looking happy as ever. His cheeks and nose were a bright cherry red, which he blamed on the cold.

Instead of handing up whatever he had for me, he decided to climb up to where I was. Each step that he took seemed to make him teeter, until he finally got up to my bunk and thumped down on it. He reached into his back pocket and pulled out a melted, bent, and half eaten Better Bar.

"Uhm… thanks," I said, not too sure if I even wanted to eat it.

"OK, never mind then," he answered in a tone just below screaming, then threw the candy to the floor.

I was too confused to really do or say anything. I just sat and watched as he climbed back down and plopped into his bed. When I asked what was wrong, there was no answer, just a few grumbles and the sound of him turning in his bed. I was about to hop down and talk to him face to face, but then Chelsea and Tommy came into the room. Chelsea was so excited to see me, which was very sweet, but also very annoying. Thankfully, Tommy came and pulled her into her bed before I had to ask her to leave me alone.

"Guy sleeps a lot, huh?" he said, looking at Donnie.

Donnie rolled over with a groan and stuck out his hand. Tommy shook it, they introduced themselves, and Donnie even said hello to Chelsea. Then he said, "There, now you don't need to bother me anymore." He rolled back over, leaving Tommy in a state of confusion, just like me.

The next few days were very similar. Donnie would be himself in the mornings, but a drunken and angry fool at night. I would spend my days with Rebeca, either cleaning or shooting, or both. She was so tough most of the time, but I'd catch certain moments where she acted like she must've before all this. Sometimes I saw a genuine smile, or a laugh, or a joke. It was almost like she had mastered the tough act, but it was slowly cracking. She even had me practice climbing the wall to figure out how to maneuver on it in case we had to get out through the ceiling.

One day when I was practicing my shooting, the Pukes noticed us and marched up to the gate. Rebeca killed most of them, but not all. She told me it was time that I killed a monster. I had a perfect view of them and the gun was fully loaded, but I couldn't shoot. The closer one got to the fence, the more vivid their face became. It was a girl. Beautifully long, brown hair was tied back in a ponytail and rested on her chestnut skin. I couldn't kill her. She was a monster now, but what if there was a cure out there and we were taking their life from them? What if I could get Taylor back? I was sure the rest of the world would be happy knowing that their loved ones were still out there when a cure came. How could I rob them of that?

Rebeca exhaled loudly and put her back to the fence. "It's either that thing out there, or me," she said. "One of us is dying today."

"Stop!" I screamed, but that only made it move a little faster toward Rebeca.

"Make a call," she said as she closed her eyes.

With each new thudding beat of my heart, my vision tunneled in. I knew I had to kill it, or it was going to turn Rebeca. I was going to kill it. I had to kill it. I fired and the Puke fell onto its back. I walked over and kept shooting till my gun clicked, and even then, I kept pulling the trigger. Rebeca came over and ripped the gun from my hands.

"It's okay," she whispered. "You got it. It can't hurt us, and it isn't in pain anymore."

The girl was laid out on the frosted ground. Her green eyes stared up at me. She coughed as the creature crawled out from her mouth and died inches away from us. The gaping hole in her throat was the size of a softball. She let out a long sigh as her eyes rolled to the back of her head and she got to let go.

The day was still young, but Rebeca told me to head in and rest. Before I took a step, I surveyed my body and it felt normal. It was like I'd just shot at a practice target again. My hands trembled a bit, but that was mostly from the recoil. I hadn't thought I'd feel like this. I was happy that I'd killed the Puke, but mostly that I'd been able to pull the trigger at all.

My ears were still ringing as I walked back into the mall. There were some muffled noises behind me, then a hand grabbed my shoulder. It made me jump; I swung my arms towards whoever it was. I turned around and saw Les, who had his hands blocking the place I'd hit before.

"I tried to call out to you, but I guess you didn't hear me. Thank God I learned from last time we tried this," he said with a smile.

I told him what happened outside and that I was going to my room to try and relax a bit. He patted my shoulder and told me how brave I'd been for killing the Puke, and that it really showed that I could be trusted to defend the mall if they needed me. After thanking him, I headed to my store. Just before I got away from him, he said that Chelsea was already in there, so I shouldn't plan on resting too much too soon.

Just like he'd said, as soon as I stepped foot into the room, Chelsea was on me talking a mile a second about things I couldn't care less about. She started with a story of a squirrel she'd seen, then talked about a hunt she'd been on with Tommy, but she'd scared all the animals away before he could shoot. I was playing along, standing and talking with her, but eventually, when I could tell that it wasn't going to end, I gently pushed by her and climbed into my bed. That didn't stop her from talking to me, but after hearing her voice for so long, it became like white noise.

There were forty-eight tiles on the ceiling. Since I couldn't sleep, I figured I'd count them. I thought it'd make me fall asleep, but nope. Instead, I reached the number forty-eight about eleven times before it gave me a headache. I closed my eyes to try and relieve the pressure on my head, and moved the pillow to try and block out some of Chelsea's talking. All I focused on was my heartbeat. The thudding sound of blood being pushed through me was soothing. That was until a thud from outside the room was loud enough to make Chelsea go quiet. I opened my eyes and looked at her and her scared face. She whispered that there had been a gunshot inside the mall.

CHAPTER 9

I hopped down from my bunk and peaked out into the hall. Three men dressed in all black were walking through the mall. They each had a shotgun and one was pushing Rebeca forward with theirs. Each room they'd enter was searched from top to bottom before moving on to the next. Before they entered ours, Chelsea grabbed me and pulled me to the back of the store. She tapped on the wall a few times, then a large chunk of it fell out and revealed a space large enough for us to squeeze into.

The two men who weren't holding Rebeca at gunpoint walked into the room and started searching. When they pulled my bunk away from the wall, at least ten empty bottles fell to the floor. One of the men started laughing and said they knew they were in the right place.

"Donnie boy!" one of the men shouted. "Let's make this easy and you come out with that little one you got!"

Chelsea's eyes widened as she scanned my body. I could see the worry on her face, but it was matched with a look like I'd lied to her. I'd have loved to explain who they were and what was happening, but I had no idea myself. Besides, I couldn't worry about what she thought of me, I had more important things to be concerned about.

I desperately wanted to find a gun, so I told Chelsea to stay where she was and I left to head to the supply room. The men walked out of our store and headed for the back door, so I made a break down the hall. By the front door, the light reflected off a set of keys. I took a second to thank God after I'd scooped them up, then ran to get a gun. After picking one, I began tiptoeing towards the main hall. My throat grew tight and my hands were clammy, slipping all over the grip. A large boom came from the back door as the three men kicked it in, now holding Les, Tommy, and Rebeca at gunpoint. I ducked behind one of the pillars and waited for some sort of opening so I could do something.

"Now, I'm only going to ask once!" one man yelled. "Come out and we won't kill them!"

After a moment's pause with no response, the men started walking down the hall with their captives, saying they'd kill one person each time they needed to waste another breath. They walked in front of my store, and Chelsea must've seen Tommy because she ran out and hugged him. It looked like she was going to get herself killed by doing that since one of the men jumped back and aimed his gun down at the back of her head. Tommy noticed and stood quickly, reaching for the gun. The other man beat the side of his head and threw him back to the ground.

"All right, have it your way!" the man said as he placed the barrel against Tommy's head.

I had to act, to do something. I aimed and pulled the trigger. The bullet struck the man's shoulder less than a second before he shot. His bullet landed inches from Tommy's skull. I took cover as they returned fire. It was my first time being shot at directly, and it made me panic. I couldn't catch my breath and my eyes darted around the mall as I tried to find a way out.

Their shooting stopped as they started coming my way. Each step landed with a boom, and it just kept getting louder in my ears. I had to move, but my knees were locked in place. I knew I was going to die, but I had to disable at least one of them before I did. I shifted my weight so that as soon as one of their legs popped out, I could litter it with bullets. They wouldn't be able to leave this place in the same condition as when they'd entered, and that was good enough for me.

Finally, the tip of a silky black boot shined in my eyes. I thought about blowing his toes off, but I wanted to make it really hurt, not just sting. I lined my gun up with the place his leg would be and waited. Before another step could be taken, cold metal touched the top of my head. I'd been so focused on shooting his leg, I hadn't seen him snake his body around the pillar and place the gun to my head. He didn't say a word, just smiled like a shark. The trigger creaked as he began applying pressure. There was no way I'd be able to fight back without a bullet in my skull before I moved an inch. He'd got me, and we both knew it. I closed my eyes and waited to be with my family again.

The pop of the gunshot rang in my ears, but I felt no pain. I opened my eyes to see blood squirting out of the man's neck like a fountain. The front door had swung open, and Donnie was standing in the doorway, smoke draining out of his gun. The remaining two men started firing at him, but he tucked himself back behind the door. I quickly peaked back around the pillar to see if Rebeca, Les, Tommy, or Chelsea were dead, but they were all still alive. They huddled together, hot shell casings raining down around them.

Since all the invaders' attention was on the front door, I took the opportunity to pop off a few shots of my own. One bullet hit one of the men in his knee, dropping him. I lined up another shot with the last man standing's head, but when I pulled the trigger, the bullet flew into Rebeca's left arm. She let out a scream which distracted the shooter. In the chaos, Donnie stormed in and shot the man with several bullets to the chest.

As the smoke started to clear, the backdoor flew open.

Kevin, Monty, and Ralph stormed in and stripped the gun from the one shooter still alive and beat him. Then they carried Rebeca to the medical store, with Les following behind them. Erica and Peter ran out to check on Tommy and Chelsea. Tommy's face was a wet crimson mask, and Chelsea was crying over him like he'd died.

Donnie ran over and gave me a quick, tight hug. I could smell booze on him, but at that point I didn't care. Then, he jogged over to the man on the ground and threw his whole body behind the punch that landed on the man's jaw. Kevin and the others came back to get the man, who was now snoring like a boar, and brought him into the medical room too. I asked why they'd help treat him. They said it was to make sure he would recover so they could make him talk. Donnie pulled out his canteen and took a few chugs, followed by a long exhale like a dragon breathing fire, then went with Kevin.

I went to check on Tommy, who was now standing and being bandaged by Erica and Peter. Their kids were on the ground by them, and they kept having to pick them up before they crawled away. When I got there, they seemed overjoyed to see me and asked if I could bring the kids into the daycare for a bit. I picked up both babies, but when I started walking, someone grabbed my hand. It was Chelsea, eyes swollen and red. Tommy told me to take her with me so she could get her mind off everything. We went to the daycare and I started to play with Jillian and Anthony, but Chelsea just stood in the corner and stared. Her silence was so off-putting, I couldn't focus on anything else.

"Come play with us, Chelsea," I said with high energy. She still didn't respond.

Anthony reached for me, so I lifted him in my arms and tickled his plump stomach. As I played with him, Jillian started fussing at the front of the store. I looked to see her reaching up to Chelsea but getting nothing in response. I went over and hoisted Jillian up and put both babies behind a small gate. I called out to Chelsea but there was no response. I started to get close to her when I noticed that she was shaking and scratching at her arms to the point where they had started bleeding. I grabbed her hands and told her to stop, but all she did was stare at me with an emotionless face.

"You know we are all going to die," she said, so matter-of-factly that it sent a chill rocketing up my spine. There were a few seconds of silence as I tried piecing together what to say in response, but she spoke before I could. "I... I don't wanna die, Alex."

There was no other option but to hug her. She turned to jelly in my arms and wept bitterly. Her crying made both babies join in, and before I knew it, the entire store had turned into one large, pitiful sight. I thought about crying with them. Before the world fell apart, I'd cry to make myself feel better. But when I tried, no emotion came to me. All I felt was heaviness in my chest and hollowness in my stomach.

The crying didn't last long as Tommy, Erica and Peter came in just after it started. Erica and Peter went over to Jillian and Anthony, and Tommy came up to me and Chelsea. As soon as she saw him, Chelsea peeled away from me and hugged him. Tommy mouthed a 'thank you' to me, and steered her out of the room.

CHAPTER 10

Erica and Peter were whispering amongst themselves so I wanted to go and make sure they were okay too. They seemed surprised that I'd come to check on them, but they were just as appreciative. I asked if they knew what had happened, and they didn't seem to know much.

"All I heard was a bang," Erica said. "Then there were men holding a gun to Rebeca's head. They saw us and said if we tried to run, they'd kill our babies, so we huddled down in here."

"We just did what they said," Peter added. "If something were to happen to one of my family... I-I don't know what I'd do... Everything seems pointless without them."

I reached out and gave them both a hug, then knelt down to Jillian and Anthony and gave them a kiss before heading out to check on the people in the medic store.

Donnie was standing over the man when he woke up from being knocked out. It took a few seconds for him to regain himself, then he looked straight at Donnie and said that they'd found us. Without missing a beat, Donnie pulled out his pistol and put a hole between the man's eyes. Everyone in the room flooded around him and the gun was ripped from his hands. Monty and Ralph pinned him against the wall as Rebeca and Les hollered. When Donnie noticed Les, he attempted to charge at him. I ran and stood in front of Donnie to get him to calm down. The sight of me seemed to do just that, as he went limp in Ralph and Monty's arms. Kevin ordered for him to be put inside the holding store so he could cool off. As he was being taken away, Donnie looked at me with a slight smile on an otherwise expressionless face. The people in the room started questioning me like I'd know why he'd done that.

"Who is he?" Rebeca demanded from her bed.

I didn't know what to say to her, or what those men had been looking for. I crept over to the body as if he was merely sleeping and studied him. Even with blood bubbling through the skull, I recognized him. He was one of the people who'd been with Georgie when they'd slaughtered my parents. I stumbled back while my eyes rolled from side to side, but snatched the edge of the bed to keep myself upright.

"So, you do know him?" Les asked.

"He killed my parents… Then I was their prisoner…" I eked out.

The mood in the room changed when I spoke. It went from tense and angry, to quiet, and almost guilty. Kevin broke the silence and told me that I should go rest, but I knew I wouldn't be able to. On my way to the room, I met eyes with Donnie. Blood splattered his face and chest, but that didn't stop him from smiling and waving to me. I gave a hesitant wave back, then dipped into my store. Tommy and Chelsea were in the room, and they asked what the gunshot had been. All I could say was that Donnie had killed the killer. They both looked surprised, but Chelsea looked slightly happy about it, like the monster in her closet had moved out.

Without saying anything else, I climbed up to my bunk. The bottles that spilled out from behind Donnie's bed were in a garbage bin out in the hall, but the sight of them turned my stomach. I needed to put my foot down about Donnie's drinking because he wasn't the same man who had saved my life.

I was unbelievably tired, but my mind wouldn't shut off. The way Donnie killed that man reminded me of the way Georgie killed my mother. He'd been quick and made it seem easy. It was like killing was the solution to a math problem that no one else got but them. The faces of my parents, the man Donnie had just shot, and the man I'd killed all flashed through my mind. So much death, so much gone in the blink of an eye, or the twitch of a finger. I wrapped my arms around myself and shivered at the thought that I could be the next to go. I might die from becoming a monster, having my brains blown out, starvation, thirst, disease, or burning. I'd be thrown to the wayside, no one caring enough to remember me. That revelation filled me with fear but also a touch of joy. If I died, I wouldn't have to fight anymore. Everything happening was irrelevant since we were all just functioning corpses, each waiting to finally get the chance to stop trying.

I was so far down my own pit of thought that I didn't realize the person who climbed up next to me till I felt their hot air on my neck. I scooted back in my bed, grabbed them by the throat and balled up my fist. Thankfully, I realized it was Chelsea before I hit her. She shuddered and asked if she could sleep next to me. Normally, I would've been weirded out by it, but not that night; it was exactly what I wanted. She didn't touch me at all, but just having someone next to me was enough.

I couldn't handle the idea of going to bed without checking on Donnie. As Chelsea got herself situated, I told her I needed to take care of something. I jumped out and took a look down the hall. Kevin stood in front of the cage, talking to Donnie, and Donnie seemed pretty happy about it. He looked at me over Kevin's shoulder and gave me an almost ironic smile, without teeth and closed eyes. Kevin told me that Donnie would be fine and that I should get rest.

Chelsea was already asleep when I crept back into bed. That night, the nightmares woke me a few times, but when they did, having Chelsea by me gave me peace of mind. Daybreak came faster than it had any other night since the outbreak. For the first time, Rebeca's marching steps woke me and she came in before I was ready to go out. Her arm was bandaged and held up in a sling. She asked if I was okay with being at the front or if I wanted to take a day off. How could I not go with her after finding out that the people who'd attacked us were looking for Donnie? Besides, she'd need me if something were to happen.

As we headed out, I looked toward the holding store, but Donnie wasn't there. I started to panic before I asked Rebeca where he was moved to. She assured me that he was still there, just curled up behind the counter, sleeping.

Most of the morning at the gate was quiet, with only a few comments here and there – mostly me apologizing for shooting Rebeca's arm. After some time had passed, I wondered why Donnie and the scavenging group hadn't left yet. Rebeca explained that they'd decided to stay at the mall for the next few days. They wanted to make sure that more people wouldn't come and that we'd have as much defense as possible in case they did.

She stood from her chair and said it was time I learned how to defend myself without using a gun. I stood across from her as she charged at me. Sticking my arms out to try and push her back did nothing but allow her to spin me around with them. She wrapped her arms around my back and almost lifted me off my feet.

"Now try grabbing me like that," she said after releasing me.

I sprinted at her and planned on paying her back for grabbing me, but I ended up face down and struggling to breath. Rebeca lifted me back to my feet and apologized for hitting me so hard.

"Now imagine I had a weapon in my hand instead of just a fist," she said.

I acted like I was trying to understand, but only to give myself time to catch my breath. She called me out by saying I didn't have a clue what she'd done, and I agreed. Her explanation was a bit all over the place as she bounced from detail to detail, but I was able to pick most of it up. She'd stepped out with her right foot, slid her left, and used the momentum to twist her hips and throw a fist into my chest.

I tried over and over to get it right, but something was always missing. I'd stumble over my feet on the slide. I'd be too slow and end up getting grabbed anyway. Or, what happened most often: I'd step the wrong way and look like a fool. She wasn't too harsh on me for not getting it, but she did tell me to try and remember it. She sat back down in her chair and I practiced for a bit longer, then went to sit with her.

"You know, Kevin was the one who found this place," Rebeca said as we studied the horizon. "Before long, people started coming and he was too good of a man to turn them away. But with all those mouths to feed and all of them looking to one person to lead, he needed some help."

She went on to explain that once she'd found the mall, Kevin had just made some people leave the day before and was riddled with guilt. Rebeca made a system that if you don't help, you don't stay. She'd had tons of people kicked out without Kevin having to. She said that because of her taking most of the responsibility, Kevin was able to be nonchalant about things that he probably shouldn't have been.

Before long, our time outside was done and we were waiting to be relieved by Erica or Peter. Minute after minute went by, but no one came. It was odd for them to make us wait for so long, so Rebeca told me to stay while she checked on them. It only took a minute for her to come back out and say that they weren't coming. Apparently, they were too scared to leave Jillian and Anthony alone after what had happened the day before. I guess I couldn't blame them, but the fact that they'd sit and cower instead of actively defending the building they lived in made me pretty mad.

"Well... I guess we are in for a long day," I said, trying to lighten the mood.

"No, I want you to go in and get Les to come out with me."

I didn't want to leave her, but she seemed pretty dead-set on me getting Les, so eventually I did what she asked. I ran to the back of the mall, noticing that Tommy and Chelsea were still in our store. I gave them a thumbs up to check if they were good and Tommy gave me a nod to say that everything was okay. Just before I walked out the back door, I looked in on Donnie and saw his feet poking out from behind the counter. I smacked the cage, to see if he'd move, and he did but only to make a small adjustment. The cage was locked down to the floor; before I let Les go out front, I was going to get his keys.

"Afternoon, Alex," Les said as I opened the door. Erica, Peter and the babies were out with him.

"Rebeca needs you to help her out front today," I said, staring at the pair.

"I don't know if I like that," Les said. "Her staying awake that long can't be healthy for her."

I didn't know how to respond, so I just told him that she wouldn't take no for an answer from me, but maybe he'd have better luck. He smiled and told me that there was as slim of a chance of that happening as a snowflake falling in Hell.

We walked back into the mall, leaving the others outside. I asked him for the keys to Donnie's cage, and said I wanted to check on him to make sure he was okay. He said that Kevin had been checking on him all morning so he was definitely fine, but if it would make me feel better, he was okay with it. He reached out with keys in hand, and told me to make sure I got them back to him when I was done. I thanked him, then went and unlocked the cage.

Sliding it up didn't wake Donnie, just made him roll around a bit. I got a good look at him and saw that his body was surrounded with small empty alcohol bottles. His shirt and pants were both partially off like he was trying to get undressed but gave up halfway. He was mumbling something between his snores, which sounded like he was calling out to me, so I went and nudged him.

"I told you to never wake me like that!" he shouted, throwing me back in fear.

"D-Donnie, it's me, Alex."

He didn't respond, just shot me a look, then thudded his head back down. I didn't know what to do or how to act, if I was supposed to wake him again, or just leave him be. As I was thinking, Kevin's voice rang out behind me, telling me to give him a few hours so he could wake up.

There didn't seem to be anything else for me to do, so I went back to the store to try and sleep some more. When I walked in, Chelsea was curled up on her bed, and Tommy knelt next to her. He was rubbing her shoulder, seemingly trying to comfort her. She saw me and came over to give me a hug. Her body was shaking and sweating when her arms wrapped around me. When I asked what was wrong, she told me that she'd had a bad dream that everyone was dead, and when she woke to see me not next to her, she'd thought it had come true. She buried her head back into my shoulder and kept her cry as quiet as she could.

I wanted to make her feel better, but I couldn't think of anything to do. Scanning the room, I noticed my bag on the floor, with a small, stuffed foot sticking out. I told Chelsea to go sit so I could get a surprise for her. I ran over and pulled out the Amy doll that Donnie and I had found a few weeks before. Chelsea had her head in her hands when I brought the doll to her, but as soon as she saw it, her face lit up like the sun. She asked if it was for her, and when I said it was, she ripped it from my hands and clutched it with a joyous squeak. Tommy told Chelsea how nice it was, and that she should go show Erica, Peter, and the kids. She went skipping out of the room with the Amy doll still clasped to her chest.

"Thanks for that, Alex," Tommy said with a smile, "I can tell that meant a lot to her." I told him not to worry about it, and that I was happy to make her happy. A smile stretched across his face and he looked almost as happy as Chelsea.

Before I could say anything else, Chelsea came back into the room and said it was time for dinner. Thankfully, she seemed to have bounced back to normal because when we sat down to eat in the kitchen, she was the one doing all the talking. She mostly said how loveable and pretty the Amy doll was, while Tommy and I nodded and grunted at her in agreement. The three of us walked back to our store and found Donnie curled up in his bed.

He was still sleeping, but just having him back in the store gave me a sense of relief. I went to give him a kiss on the cheek, but saw they were both wet. He looked up at me and said that he loved me, and I told him that I loved him too.

It was so nice to get into bed, but it made me think about Rebeca. She was still outside and would be throughout the night.

I felt so bad for her, so I decided that I was going to take over for her tomorrow so she could relax. Maybe if Donnie felt up to it, he could come out with me. It felt like I hadn't seen him, the real him, in a long time.

CHAPTER 11

Cracks of light peaked through the winter clouds and woke me. Not that I was deep in sleep anyway, but I was getting close. Tommy and Chelsea were still in bed, but when I peeked down to see Donnie, he was gone. I walked into the hall, fearful that he'd be locked up again, but he wasn't. Erica and Peter were up so I asked them if they'd seen Donnie. According to them, he'd headed down to the cafeteria. I walked in to see him standing in a far corner of the room. He was too busy filling his pockets and backpack with different types of booze to notice me until I called out to him.

"M-mornin', Alex," he slurred in a voice painful to listen to.

I tried to stay calm, but there was no way to. "Why, Donnie? Drinking this shit has changed you. It's like you're not even the same person anymore."

He didn't say anything, just blinked and turned back to gathering alcohol. My demand that he stop and talk to me did nothing. I needed him to listen to me. He owed me that. I ran over and pulled on his arm. He spun on his heels and shoved me to the floor. There was silence, then I guess he realized who I was and what he'd done.

"A-Alex... do not do that... please," he said slowly as tears flooded over his glazed eyes.

He helped me to my feet, then walked out of the kitchen with me following behind. Tommy and Chelsea were waking up as we walked back into our store. We smiled, and Donnie was even able to say good morning without sounding like he'd forgotten his tongue. Chelsea ran up to show us her doll, and Donnie raised his eyebrows and smiled like he was actually interested.

As we were talking, Rebeca and Les walked in. Donnie's happy demeanor disappeared as soon as he noticed Les. Donnie stormed up to get in his face, and demanded that we be left alone. Les recoiled after every word that Donnie snapped, which was probably due to the shower of spit that flew in his face.

"I will leave," Les conceded. "But just so you know, I can smell the alcohol on your breath."

Donnie balled up his fists and clenched his teeth. Before he could swing and hurt Les, or get himself hurt, I ran between them. I begged him to stop and go lay down before he did something he couldn't change. He looked down at me, puckered his lips, then flopped down in his bed. I took a moment to thank God, then looked back at the pair and waited for them to tell me what I was doing for the day.

Rebeca looked like a train had run over her after a car. She said that I was going to be with her, and Tommy and Chelsea would go with Les. Chelsea ran to me and said that she was going to teach Amy how to garden. I told her that after she taught Amy, Amy could teach me, which made her chuckle. She skipped out of the room, and Tommy followed behind. Before Les could go too, I pulled him away from Rebeca and asked what had happened the night before.

"Seems you were right," he said with an unenthusiastic smile. "She would not let me stay with her. I did come to check on her a few times, but besides that she's been alone."

I thanked him for trying as we went our separate ways. Catching up with Rebeca was easy since she was dragging her feet towards the front door. Her eyes were droopy and sunk into her head. Her injured arm was out of its sling, and along with the other, they swung like overdone noodles at her sides. When we finally got outside, she threw herself into the chair and continued watching out on the horizon. "I used to stay up for days before all this shit started," she said. "It's never been so hard to do before."

"That's probably because if you fell asleep before, you knew you'd wake up so there was no pressure... That's not the case now."

Just as I was getting ready to tell her that I'd take over, the front door flew open. Kevin, Monty, Ralph, and eventually Donnie, came out. I was shocked to see Donnie going out to scavenge, and I went to tell Kevin it wasn't the best idea. After I'd whispered it to him, he looked at me like I was crazy and shook his head.

"Donnie's a good and trustworthy guy. He just needs to shake it off, and he'll quickly do that," Kevin responded.

From the tone of his voice, and the look that Donnie was giving me, I could tell that trying to convince them was pointless. Donnie gave me a pat on the back of my head, then the four of them headed out.

Rebeca slid me my gun and told me to keep watch so she could rest a bit. She joked about Les wanting to help, but since he was an awful shot, she was better off staying awake and taking care of everything herself. The fact that she trusted me to take a shot made me feel pretty good.

The sound of Pukes crying in the distance made me wonder if they were making that sound because they were in pain, if they were being forced to, or a combination of both. The thought made me rethink the idea of wanting them to stay alive in case of a cure. Now I thought that it may be better to just kill them. That's what I'd want.

Since I was deep in thought, I almost missed the fact that there was movement on the horizon. It looked like a person was running at us, and I thought that it might be someone from the scavenging group. I started unlocking the gate. In my panic, I jostled Rebeca and she jumped up next to me. Just as the figure started to take shape, it stopped. There was no movement from it for a few seconds, until it roared like an animal going for a kill. All the Pukes cleared from the area.

"Go inside, NOW!" Rebeca demanded.

She told me to get guns and people to use them. I tried asking what the creature was, and what we were going to do, but she shoved me back and screamed for me to go. The creature was sprinting at us now, but it remained perfectly upright and entirely covered with black sludge. Rebeca screamed at me again, and this time I did as she asked.

Erica and Peter were playing with Anthony while Jillian was sleeping on the floor. I ran in and told them that a monster I'd never seen before was running towards us and Rebeca needed help. They looked at each other, then Peter ran to me and said that he knew what to do. He told me to go find the others and that he'd take care of getting guns.

Since the outbreak began, I'd experienced plenty of heartbreaking things: death, rape, beatings, killings. Never had I experienced something so heartbreaking as the sound of the daycare store's cage slamming shut behind me.

"I'm sorry," Peter muttered as he locked himself and family inside.

The feeling of betrayal was so strong that, if I tried to, I could've ripped the cage down and smashed both of their skulls in, but I didn't have the luxury of time. Gunshots started popping off, so my time had run out. There was no chance I could leave Rebeca outside, especially since I knew I had a gun, and only God knew how long it would take the others to get one. I prayed that if we did need the others, that they could be quick.

Swinging the door open, the first thing I saw was Rebeca's motionless body, standing there like nothing had happened. Joy overwhelmed me and I exclaimed that she didn't even need help. As I spoke, her head started tilting to the left. It kept going till it looked unnatural. All my joy vanished as it tumbled off her shoulders and onto the ground in front of me. The creature that I'd never seen before was standing on the other side of her, holding her up with its arm, which it had plunged into her stomach. She was one of the few people I had left and had been killed just feet from me by this disgusting, horrid thing. Another person taken from me by this world that God had turned His back on. My mind was dripping out of my nose.

There were no human parts to aim at, so I used all the ammo I had to blast this thing all over its body, but it did nothing besides make it take a few steps back. Its head moved erratically like there was a tornado swirling inside of its skull. I fired shot after shot, and I could hear it telling me I was useless. That I was going to die there and nothing and no one was going to give a shit. Rebeca's rifle was in the corner of the gated area, and I knew that if I didn't get it, I'd be dead. There was no way that I could turn and run back inside. If I did, this thing would follow. If I was able to fight it, maybe some people could get away once I failed.

It started coming towards me, barking like a dog as it moved. I threw my pistol at it then jumped for the rifle. Blood is much more slippery than you'd think. I found that out when I grabbed the rifle and it was covered in Rebeca's. My hands gripped it like a vice because of the adrenaline, but the blood made the gun slip right through my fingers. I screamed and cursed at it as the creature kept walking towards me, tilting its head and taunting me. I could not grip the damn gun, so with no other option, I laid the gun down and shot it at the creature's ankles. It seemed like a good idea at first, but the recoil sent the gun flying out of my reach, and the bullet didn't hit anything but dirt.

I couldn't help but laugh. It was like a comedy where the main character always looks like a fool no matter how simple the task. Everyone dies, and the opportunity to die had been stolen from me so many times that it felt like I was overdue. I was tired of waiting. My hope was that if I died soon enough, I'd be able to catch up with Rebeca. Then we could both meet the Maker together, and ask Him what the hell happened. That was the plan, at least.

I didn't know it, but my back was against the front door of the mall. Out of nowhere, my entire body flew to the side as it flung open, and there were several shots. It looked like they all hit the creature's knees and it collapsed to the ground next to me. I stared it in the eyes, or where I thought its eyes would be, and smiled. A barking sound rumbled in its throat as it stretched for me, but the axe that Les swung down cut that short. It took three hard chops for the thing to stop moving. I got another day, and that thing got to see me live. Bittersweet, if you ask me.

The front of the gate was smashed open and the Pukes that had just left the area began flooding in. I wasn't too concerned with them since they'd be easy enough to deal with. Rebeca was my first thought. I ran over to her head and picked it up in my hands, then placed it back on her shoulders. Les kept trying to pull me off, but I yelled for him to leave me alone. If I spent more time pushing it back on, the wound would seal, and she would just need some stitches. Tommy joined Les to pull me from

Rebeca, and I fought with all the energy I had left to stay with her, but they still drug me away.

I twirled her hair that was stuck between my fingers when they brought me back to my room. Tommy stayed behind, and Les went to clean up. My eyes were so heavy, like someone was hanging on them, but the people who came to check on me got my attention. It was Erica and Peter. They came into my room, without their kids, and asked if I was okay.

The anger I felt towards them was nauseating. I sat up in bed and screamed that they were murderers. If they'd had the courage to not be cowards for a second, maybe that would've been enough for everyone to stay alive. Instead, they'd cowered behind a cage with the flimsy excuse of protecting their family. But what about Rebeca? Was she not family to them? She'd kept them safe. I screamed that they were cowards and backstabbers.

They had the nerve to say I could go to them if I needed anything just before they walked away. The laughter that overcame me was uncontrollable. I made sure they understood that they were fools, since the last time I'd needed them, they'd gotten someone killed. They were as useful to me as the Pukes outside.

Tommy said something, but I didn't listen. I was too focused on Rebeca's hair. It had been so puffy and curly on her head, but now that I could see it up close, it was even more beautiful. As I studied it, an itch grew on my nose. The more I scratched, the more it seemed to itch. All I wanted to do was look at Rebeca's hair, but this damned itch wouldn't stop. I had to make it stop. I itched it hard, but it wouldn't stop. I had to itch this fucking spot. This fucking itch wouldn't stop.

Tommy came, grabbed my arms and I yelled how messed up that was. I explained that this itch on my face wouldn't go away and I needed to make it go away. He looked sympathetic, but still didn't let my arms go.

Chelsea came over and told me to calm down, which I thought was pretty ironic. She was the one who was always talking; I was just trying to get rid of an itch. Her eyes were swollen, tears were streaming down her cheeks, and she was clutching Amy to her chest.

"Please," she murmured, "please don't hurt yourself."

Hurt myself? I was trying to be calm by getting rid of the itch that wouldn't stop, and that's what I told them. Tommy yelled for Chelsea to get her mirror. She brought it and held it up. I didn't recognize the person looking at me. Tears, snot, and blood covered their face. They kept shaking and yelling like they were possessed. I focused on the person for a moment and realized that they did what I did; blinked when I blinked, sniffed when I sniffed. I recognized that it was me.

The mind is a wild thing sometimes. Once you're shown something revealing, it is all you can focus on. All those emotions that I hadn't allowed myself to truly feel were let lose, and there was no controlling them. My body was already enduring the storm, but it was different when it came to my brain. My eyes were like tops, spinning around and trying to find something else to focus on besides my reflection. Anger, hate, loneliness, and depression all flooded out of my skin. The pain in my head was incredible. The pain was like digging a hole that would end up being my grave. I writhed around and yelled to be let go, but then everything went black.

CHAPTER 12

"Where?" Donnie screamed, waking me from my slumber.

Chelsea was curled up next to me, and Tommy went to meet Donnie at the front of the store. I could hear Tommy struggling with him, saying that I needed to rest, but Donnie made it past him. He burst into the store, came over and scooped me up in his arms. It must've been the sleep, but my mind only then remembered and registered everything that happened. I broke down while he held me.

He asked if I was hurt, and I told him that I was fine, but that Rebeca was dead. My throat was tight as I spoke, like it was still trying to convince me it hadn't happened.

"I don't care about that. I just need to know you are okay," he replied.

My body stiffened as I pushed at him, forcing him to put me back down. He started getting angry at my lack of being able to understand what he meant. The death of others didn't bother him, only mine would. I almost chuckled at his words and said it didn't show in how he'd been acting. He was never really there, always acted as if I was the one in the wrong, and was always putting his selfish shit over me. But he said he cared, so I was just supposed to go with that?

Footsteps echoed in from the hall, which stopped me from telling Donnie what I felt. It was Les. He'd come to check on me, but of course Donnie needed to scream at him. He told Les to get out and that we didn't want him in the room. Having had enough of Donnie's 'I'm there for you until I'm not' mentality, I yelled for him to shut up. His eyes snapped back to me and his face shined with a confused expression.

Les walked past Donnie and handed me a Better Bar. "I figured that this may help, even if just a little."

I thanked him, and gave him a hug. Then I turned back to Donnie, but he was gone. The man who'd saved me was right in front of him, but Donnie couldn't even thank him. The anger I felt towards him was nauseating, even if he was drunk.

"What the hell is wrong with him?" I said. "He is a cheater, but gets mad at the guy whose wife he slept with?"

"That's what he told you?" Les asked.

I told him that I'd thought it wasn't my place to bring it up, so I'd kept quiet. He didn't say anything, just sighed and nodded.

"When we lived next to each other..." Les started. "When someone leaves the house for a long time, the people they left get... lonely."

I heard marching quickly heading our way. Donnie stormed back in with his metal canteen in hand.

"Lonely, huh?" Donnie scoffed. He walked up to Les and got close, inches from his face. "You destroyed my life," he growled.

Les took a step back and balled up his fists. "You managed that all by yourself!" he yelled.

Donnie smashed the canteen into Les's face and caused blood to flow from his mouth. Les hit Donnie back, but maybe due to the booze in his system or the fact that Les was scrawny, Donnie hardly moved. Donnie's fists cracked into Les's ribs, which made the blood already flowing from his lips shoot out like a rocket. Les started to stumble back but didn't fall. Instead, when Donnie followed him, he spit blood into his eyes. I jumped between them, but again, Donnie shoved me to the floor. This time, he screamed for me to stay out of it.

Tommy came running and also tried to separate them, but Donnie pushed him to the floor with me. That didn't stop Tommy from trying again: he jumped back up to his feet, but this time, instead of a shove, he was met with Donnie's fist. Chelsea came running and covered Tommy. The other people in the mall started poking their heads out to see what was happening, but no one did anything.

Les' face was a mangled mess of thick and flowing blood. The damage Donnie had sustained was on his fists. He had Les pressed against the wall with one arm while the other continued beating him. I screamed for it to stop as I grabbed Donnie's arm, pulling with all my strength. He howled with rage then turned and punched me in the mouth. I tumbled to the floor and held my face as the taste of warm metal flowed around my gums. The consistency made it impossible to swallow. I started to gag and spat it up on the floor.

"Oh, oh God, Alex. I'm so sorry, sweetie," Donnie said when he finally looked down at me.

He reached out to me, but Tommy smashed him in the face before he could touch me. Donnie crumbled to the floor next to me. Instead of trying to get back at Tommy, he tried to touch me. The thought of him grabbing me at all made me sick, so I kicked at him and backed away.

Tommy put his knee on Donnie's back and told him not to move. But he wasn't going to; he wouldn't have even if Tommy hadn't had his knee on him. Not because he was beaten up; instead it seemed like he'd stopped because I was mad at him. I didn't pay his sorry heap any attention; instead, I scurried over to Les. He was still on the floor, not moving much at all.

I was no doctor, but even I could tell that his nose and jaw were broken. He tried to speak, but every time he'd grimace and grab at his face. After a few attempts, he stopped trying and stared over at Donnie.

Kevin was yelling as he marched down the hall. He walked over with Monty and Ralph by his side. Kevin and Tommy scooped up Les and took him over to the medical store, while Monty and Ralph stayed behind to hold Donnie down. His eyes were still on me as he remained silent with a miserable expression across his face.

"Let the man up," Kevin instructed when he returned. "What the hell are ya thinking, beating on poor ol' Les? The hell he ever do?"

Donnie didn't respond and continued to look at me. Kevin shrugged and said that fights are normal between friends. He added that as long as it didn't happen again, there was nothing to worry about. Tommy burst out from the medical store, screaming that there was no way Donnie should stay.

"Les' face is smashed in, people are scared of this asshole, and on top of that, he punched Alex!"

Kevin looked up and smiled. "Makes me laugh when people expect others to act like life is the same as it used to be. No more government or cops, so we gotta deal with our own shit how we see fit."

Tommy's face turned bright red like the skin of a shiny new apple. He muttered that it was no wonder that Kevin couldn't run this place by himself. Kevin chuckled, then he waved to Monty and Ralph to follow him. Tommy came and helped me to my feet, then he went over to Chelsea. I looked up to see Donnie slowly walking towards me, his hands out in front of him like I was going to jump into his arms. Tommy screamed for him to keep away, then ran in front of me. I tapped him on the back and told him that it would be fine. Donnie looked so depressed that I was sure he wouldn't try to hurt me. I told Tommy to take Chelsea to the store and make sure she was okay. He said he'd be watching, before doing what I asked.

Donnie started telling me that Les was trying to get under his skin and that he'd provoked the beating he'd got. I couldn't stand hearing his excuses anymore. I interjected and told him that he was completely in the wrong, no matter what had been said between them. His face turned stiff and sour.

"If you co-could kill Georgie… you'd do it?" he asked, sounding like his words were falling down stairs.

"I'd love to," I responded.

"He's m-my… Georgie. I'm killin' him."

Dumbfounded would be an understatement for what I felt at that moment. A smile grew on his face as if he were laughing that I was upset. I was so tired of his self-pity, self-indulgence and mood swings. When I told him he needed to stop drinking, he nodded his head and marched over to our store. After a second or two, he came strolling back out, canteen in hand. He slowly unscrewed the lid, brought the bottle to his lips, took a few massive gulps, then closed it. He did it all while looking me dead in the eye. He smacked his lips together like it was the greatest thing God had put on this earth, then told me that his drink wasn't the issue. It made him think clearly and function without regret. Apparently, I was the problem because of my lack of loyalty. I asked if punching me in the face was acting without regret. He didn't give me a well-thought-out answer, just spit out that I'd already made up my mind about him so there was no point in fighting.

Kevin shouted from down the hall for Donnie to come to him, and that's what he did. It was a lost cause to try and talk while he was drunk, so I decided to save my breath and go back to my store. Tommy and Chelsea tried talking to me, but I wasn't in the mood. Rebeca's death had only just happened, but instead of being with me, Donnie had chosen to go with Kevin and his drink. It hurt, even if I didn't want to admit it.

I climbed into my bunk and curled up underneath the covers. I prayed that Les would be okay, but the issue that weighed heaviest on my heart was Donnie. I prayed that he'd return to being my hero, the man who I could be proud to look up to, the man who I'd started to love as family. A stabbing pain hit the bottom of my foot during my prayer. I snapped my head up and saw Chelsea poking me with her uncut fingernails. She didn't say anything, just climbed all the way into my bunk and gave me a hug. She'd brought the Amy doll up with her, which was nice because it reminded me of who Donnie used to be. Thinking about that and my memories with Rebeca, I finally calmed down enough to sleep.

My dreams weren't as relaxing. Georgie's smile shined like lightning cutting through dark clouds. He chuckled in my ear that everyone I loved would be dead before I knew it, and there was nothing I could do to save them. Rebeca's head rolled up to my feet, and she laughed at what a fool I was for thinking I could protect anything. She said that when she'd needed me most, I'd left her. Her eyes turned black as she started screaming at me.

"Fooooool…. You are a fool… FOOL! YOU ARE A FUCKING DIRTY FOOL!"

My body felt like it'd been dragged behind a horse when I flung myself forward out of bed. Maybe I'd have been able to fall asleep again had it not been for Donnie and Tommy screaming at each other. Each claimed that the other didn't understand or know what they were talking about. The way they yelled at one another was like a bull smashing its head into a brick wall even though it hurt like hell. They were both saying what the other did wrong, when all anyone wanted them to do was to shut the hell up.

After a while of trying my best to block out their argument, I took a peek over the ledge. Both had their fists balled, and they were so close that if they weren't arguing with each other, I'd bet they'd try to kiss. I hopped down and stood between them, hoping not to get hit again. Donnie gave me a passing glance, then went back to yelling at Tommy for getting in the way with Les. Tommy gave me an aggressive 'good morning,' but then quickly told me to move so that he could smash Donnie's teeth in. My body, my mind, and my spirit were all done with everyone's bullshit, and I was not going to have this happen in my room.

"Both of you, shut the hell up," I said, closing my eyes because of the pounding in my skull. "I can't even mourn Rebeca. Les is beat to hell. People didn't help when it could've meant saving a life… and all you're doing is arguing about which one of you is wrong. Just shut the fuck up."

They both continued debating which was more disgusting, but now they were telling me instead of each other. Just as Donnie began telling me why he was right, he paused and said that there was no point in talking to me since I'd already decided whose side to take. My body filled with such aggression towards the stupidity of his comment that it made my stomach ache.

"If you didn't drink this shit, maybe you wouldn't be so insane," I told him.

His face twisted with anger as he said, "You know nothing about insane, kid."

He'd been so mean to me, acting like I never defended him, that I wanted to laugh in his face. I wanted to make sure he understood how pissed I was at him. That was the only payback that I had in mind. Before I could, Kevin strolled in and cracked jokes about how we clearly weren't early birds since we were acting so cranky. I shot my gaze at him, but he just smiled.

"Why are ya so uptight, kiddo? You're still sucking breath, ain't ya? Be happy 'bout that."

I had no motivation to talk anymore, so I sat on Donnie's bed and listened. Tommy screamed that Donnie should be kicked out, but Kevin refused to hear it.

"I've talked it over with 'em, and we've come to an understanding," Kevin said, to Tommy's surprise. "Donnie won't do it again."

I looked at Donnie and saw him looking at the floor. He seemed like a child who'd just been punished. Kevin gave him a pat and they both walked out together. Tommy sat next to me and started rubbing his temples. What had happened didn't make sense to either one of us. There must've been something that I didn't understand about Donnie and Les that Kevin did. I was going to find out what.

"Seems like a wonderful kinda morning," Les said as he made his way into our room.

There was a piece of white tape across his newly cockeyed nose, his chin was held in place with a wrap that circled his head, and a few bandages were strewn from his face to his neck. Chelsea jumped up and gave him a hug. He told her to be careful, but it seemed to go in one ear and out the other. She slammed into his chest and squeezed, forcing a whimper of pain from him. Chelsea recoiled and apologized, but Les told her not to worry.

"After what Donnie did to me, I don't think that there is too much you could do to make it any worse," he joked.

"I actually want to talk to you about that," I told him.

He responded with a slight nod, then went back to talking with Chelsea. He said that he'd be needing all of us to help him in the garden, and that Tommy would run double duty, also guarding the front with Peter. As we headed towards the back door, I looked over to see the scavenge group – Kevin, Ralph, Monty, and Donnie – walk out without saying a word. I was happy that I didn't need to talk to Donnie again, but pissed that he'd blown me off.

When we got outside, there was a blue tarp covering something shaped like a body. A few shovels leaned up against the wall, and Les told us to start digging in the clearing. Chelsea asked what we were doing, and Les must've forgot who he was talking to because he told her the truth. It was a burial for Rebeca.

Chelsea yipped and buried her head into Tommy's chest. He tried telling her it was going to be okay but she was too busy crying to pay him any attention. I heard them behind me, but I couldn't rip my focus away from the body. The more I stared at her, the more she seemed to start breathing. I took a step to her before Les' voice yelled my name. His yell made me remember. She wasn't breathing at all. She was headless.

I turned back and started to dig with Tommy while Chelsea sat by the door with the Amy doll. The ground was frozen stiff, but it wasn't bad until Tommy had to go and work security at the front of the building. He'd leave for an hour, and during that time, I was the only one digging. We finally finished and Les told me and Tommy to drag the body over. Tommy grabbed the feet and I grabbed where the head would have been. Before I lifted, I had to see what she looked like. I could still smell her through the tarp.

Les told me not to look, that she wasn't the same, but I already knew that. I peeled back one corner and exposed her remains. Chelsea screamed and ran to the corner of the garden with Tommy following. Les' limping footsteps echoed in my ear, but my vision was fixed down on Rebeca. The slice through her neck wasn't jagged or rough, but crisp. There was black tar, which I imagined would taste like liquorish, running from the cut and down her naked body. Her once vibrant green eyes had turned to a pale, icy color. Her once creamy, chocolate skin had turned gray and purple. It was sad that she couldn't speak to me anymore, but it also amazed me how consistent she remained. Maybe death wouldn't be that bad. I mean, it couldn't be. Not if when you died, you were able to be so beautiful and pure.

Les walked in front of me and gripped my shoulder. It pulled my attention off Rebeca. He folded the tarp back over her, called Tommy, then they dumped her body into the hole. Tommy tried talking to me when he'd covered the body, but I was busy reminiscing over what I'd just seen.

Once they'd finished, Les, Tommy and Chelsea picked some potatoes and onions from the garden, then Les told the other two to go and check the front gate. They went inside and he came to sit next to me. He told me how much Rebeca had loved it in the garden. We sat in silence for a moment until he asked what I wanted to know. This snapped me from my small, self-induced daze.

"What is the truth behind how you and Donnie know each other?" I asked.

"I haven't told you anything out of respect for Donnie, as dumb as that sounds now. Actually, it's mostly respect for his family," he said, looking down at his hands. "Donnie's wife and I… we had an affair."

I went to tell him he was wrong like I knew better, but the more I thought about it, the more it made sense. Donnie's actions weren't justified, but I couldn't blame him. There was one last thing that I still didn't understand.

"Why didn't Donnie want you around me?"

Les let out a long, labored sigh. "Donnie had a daughter," he said. "She wasn't his biological daughter though... she was mine. Her name was Carly."

He explained that when Donnie had found out about the affair, he'd acted like Les had stolen his family, which, in a way, he had. So Donnie keeping Les away from me was his way of keeping his new family safe.

"So, um... what happened to his old family?" I asked as gently as possible.

"I have no idea," he said. "His wife left a few days before all this started. That seemed to make him stop drinking. As far as Carly is concerned, I was never allowed around her. I watched my daughter grow up away from me. I assumed it would be better for her if she grew up in a family that was whole instead of being bounced between two. When I saw you... I thought you were her... Clearly that isn't the case... I just hope she's okay..."

He was still looking down at his hands, now glistening with sweat, and started clearing his throat. I didn't want to ask him anything else. In a way, the woman he'd had a child with, and his child, had just died to him, and there wasn't a single thing to do. It was like we had a kinship of helplessness due to the deaths of the ones we loved.

Chelsea frantically barged out of the doors, almost falling over as she did. I jumped to my feet, ready to fight. She yelled for us to come to her, so I sprinted over, and she started digging in her pocket until she pulled out a rusty bottle cap. Relief hit me like a tsunami as I realized that this was what she was worked up about. She read a factoid off the inside of it about how many calories a person burns in a day, and she thought it was the coolest thing. She darted back inside to show the babies in the daycare, and it made Les and I laugh to see how excited she was about something so minor. It was nice to see.

Both of us picked up the food and were heading inside when I crunched down on the freshly dug up dirt. My mind started drifting to Rebeca again, but there was another thought that echoed: what happened to the thing that killed her? I asked Les, and he told me they'd lit it on fire, and it had melted away like ice in the sun. All that was left were some bits of mangled flesh and bones.

We got back inside, and I started shuffling down the hall, wondering when Donnie would return. I got my answer when I saw him heading into the kitchen. Les and I walked in, placed the vegetables on the table, then I made a beeline to Donnie. I tried making small talk by asking where he'd gone, and if he'd found anything good, but he acted like I wasn't there.

"I've done nothing to you, but you think I'm the one in the wrong?" I asked.

An arrogant smile grew to cover his face. What more could I expect from him at this point? The Donnie I knew was lost, and I wasn't having any luck bringing him back. I asked for him to at least look at me when I talked, which he did. I asked if he was still drinking, and he continued silently smiling as he looked away again. He was right; I already knew.

"It's funny," I said. "You're a functional drunk…"

I could feel his anger grow after I spoke and regained his full attention. "You think you're real smart, huh?" he barked, which made me shine with a smile of my own as I nodded. "You're nothing but a dumb little bitch… Now leave me alone."

I thought that if I was rougher with him, it'd make him

realize how different he'd been. Instead, I was told to leave, but that was all I needed to hear to know that the Donnie I'd once known and cared for wasn't there.

Les interjected himself and said that he was sorry for what had happened the day before. He stuck out his hand to Donnie, but Donnie didn't take it. He looked Les up and down with flared nostrils. I was getting prepared for another fight, and this time I wouldn't be so nice about getting Donnie off. But that didn't happen. Donnie let out a sharp exhale and pushed his way past Les and out of the store. Les smiled and said he guessed that was a start, but his hands were trembling.

We walked back to my store, where Chelsea and Tommy were already sitting. Just as I went to sit down, Erica called that dinner was ready. For the first time, Chelsea seemed too tired to do anything. We told her to wait behind and we'd bring her food.

CHAPTER 13

The smell coming from the cafeteria was horrid, like burnt hair and chemicals. There was a boiling pot on the stove and Donnie was standing in front of it. Kevin stuck a pair of tongs into the pot and pulled out a hunk of pale-colored meat. The disgust I felt must've shown on my face because Kevin told me not to worry, and that it was just chicken being cooked. Hesitantly, I walked forward to get myself a bowl and Kevin scooped me out a massive chunk and smacked it down. I thanked him and started walking away. I heard Tommy walk up after me to get himself and Chelsea some food, but this time when Kevin placed meat into the bowl, it dropped with a crash. I chuckled as I turned to call Tommy butterfingers, but his face was white and he was staring down at the shattered glass. Long, jagged teeth were littered across the floor, along with a single, shriveled eye.

My body flung itself backwards and my bowl crashed onto the ground. I demanded to know what we were eating. Kevin smiled at us and said it was a dog. My mouth ran like a broken faucet as I got ready to throw up.

"We were running low on food, and Donnie knew that we had to kill something, so he found this," Kevin added.

Donnie was smiling in the corner of the room, and when I saw how happy he was, I stormed out. Secretly serving us dog meat was almost like a practical joke to them. Once I got into the hall, I heard slamming steps behind me before Donnie's voice boomed.

"Hey!" he hollered. "You've gotta eat… now!"

I didn't care and blew him off as I walked back into my store. He ran into the room, snatched me by the arm and started pulling me back towards the kitchen. I kicked and yelled for him to let me go, but he was so strong. Les and Tommy ran towards us, and Tommy grabbed Donnie while Les pulled me away. Tommy was able to hold him by forcing his arms backwards, but that did nothing to stop Donnie from trying to move. He was screaming and thrashing around to be let go. Kevin rushed out and started pulling Tommy off Donnie. Once he was freed, he started running at me and Les. I was scared that he was going to start hitting us, but there was nowhere I could run. I planted my feet and waited for the first blow.

"SHE ISN'T CARLY!" Les cried out, making Donnie freeze. "My Carly is dead… Isn't that right, Donnie? She's dead?"

Donnie shook his head at the floor before looking up again. He had tears rolling down his cheeks that came to rest in his unkempt beard. He started to get closer, but Les stood in front of me. His fists were so tightly balled that his knuckles turned white and shook like a small dog. I gave him a pat and told him that I'd be fine. He didn't move, but he let me go ahead of him.

Donnie outstretched his hand, which made me flinch and close my eyes. I paused and wondered when the blow would come, but he only caressed my cheek with the back of his rough hand. His eyes watered as he stared at me, then continued walking past us and into our store. Tommy came over to check on me and Les. Kevin told some joke before heading back into the kitchen. It was quiet and felt like the calm that comes after a storm, but it didn't last long.

Smashing started coming from our store. I ran over with Les

and Tommy behind me, and we saw Donnie flinging bottles of alcohol around the room. Chelsea was on her bunk, hiding under her covers. Tommy jumped onto the bunk to shield her from the flying glass, and I ran to Donnie to make him stop. What had once been a few streams of tears had turned into an ocean. He wept bitterly and when I tried to pull him away to calm down, he fell onto the floor and started smashing his fist into the broken glass.

"COWARD! FUCKING COWARD!" he screamed, like a man gone insane.

I wrapped my arms around him and squeezed as tight as I could, telling him he needed to calm down. He paused and turned to me with a face of pure sorrow.

"I hate it all so fucking much," he cried.

He started smashing his fists into the glass again, and I couldn't hold him back. Les came over so I blocked Donnie to keep them from fighting again. He returned my gesture by giving me a pat on the back before he moved past me. I waited and watched with my breath caught in my throat. Les knelt down and sternly called out to Donnie.

"Tell me what happened with Carly," Les asked in a whisper. "Please, tell me what happened to her… I have to know."

Donnie looked up at him, unable to stop his lips from quivering into an awfully pitiful frown. "She's… she's dead."

"How?" Les asked, his face beginning to grow distorted.

"S-she was sick. She wouldn't eat. Georgie wouldn't let us in… We were surrounded by the monsters, but she wouldn't stand…" Donnie said in an agonized voice. "She was still looking at me to help her… She was so heavy. I pulled my gun, but… but her eyes, those beautifully green eyes, they wouldn't let me end it for her."

"You left her?" Les questioned.

Donnie nodded with a sob.

Les' face stretched like it was going to slip off his skull. He looked at me, then planted his right shin into Donnie's skull. Before anyone could react, Les was on top of Donnie, beating his face in, but Donnie didn't fight back. He just stayed there, arms outstretched, and took it.

I screamed for Les to stop, and Tommy went to pull him off, but it was like he had been possessed; he threw Tommy away. If I didn't act, Donnie would die. No one else was doing anything, so I ran and smashed my body into Les, making him tumble onto his side. Tommy climbed on top of him, then Kevin followed suit as he rushed in. Les kept screaming, but it wasn't words, just aggression.

Donnie was motionless on the floor, muttering about how sorry he was. I ran down to the medical store and picked up some bandages. When I got back, Les was sitting in the hall with his head in his hands. I gave some of the bandages to Tommy then headed back to Donnie. Les screamed for me to leave that "cowardly murderer" to die, but I couldn't.

The store was silent. Donnie was outstretched on his bunk, motionless. I started walking towards him and he started tracking me with his eyes until I sat down. Before I could do anything, he leaned over the side of the bed and started throwing up. When he was done, I took up a rag and cleaned his face.

"I'm no good, sweetie," he whispered as he dropped his head back down on the bed.

"I know."

Donnie was just about cleaned up when Tommy came and yanked him from the bed. I told him he didn't need to be so rough with him.

"He's going to the holding room tonight," Tommy said. "Then he's leaving in the morning."

We reached the holding room and Tommy threw Donnie in, making him land on his head. When he went to close the gate, I stood under it and told him that Donnie should sleep in his bed. It would be easier if he was there.

"How long have you known him?" Tommy said.

I told him we had been together for a couple of months, and during that time, he saved my life more than once.

"What makes you think that he wouldn't sacrifice you to save himself?" he asked, and I had no answer. "We cannot have cowards like him living here. People like him are too risky."

He pulled me away and slammed the gate closed. I ran back and told Donnie that everything would be figured out, he just needed to give me some time. He looked at me with a blank expression before curling up on the floor. The emotions that I felt towards Donnie were still there, the anger and neglect, but now I just wanted him to be okay.

"I want him gone! He has to be gone by tonight!" I could hear Les demanding from down the hall.

Kevin was saying that wasn't going to happen, and that they would figure it out in the morning.

"What the hell are you so protective over him for?" Les yelled.

After a few seconds, he said, "I knew 'bout all this. He told me a few weeks ago."

Everyone around him looked shocked that he wouldn't have said anything to anyone about it.

"He said he abandoned Carly, that he wanted to kill her but couldn't, and that he drinks so he doesn't have to see her face when he closes his eyes."

Les stormed at Kevin, fueled by his newly revealed aggression, but Tommy held him back. Kevin was expressionless, even as Les swung punches inches from his face.

"He reminded me of myself," Kevin added, "I had to watch people die as soon as I kicked 'em from here. I saw 'em when I tried to sleep. After some time, I was able to work my way through it and accept that this world had no place for weakness anymore. That's what I thought I was helping Donnie to do: work through it."

"Donnie hasn't been himself," I said. "He started drinking again just before we got here. I would've stopped him if I knew his history, but maybe it helped at first."

"No, it didn't! He's just a fucking drunk!" Les hollered. "Why do you think his wife came to me? He used to drink, then beat her, then drink some more."

"That means you're just as guilty!" I said, trying to scrape together some kind of defense. "Instead of keeping Donnie's wife away from him, you slept with her and sent her back! You're a hypocrite."

The room was silent before Les spoke again. "If you feel that way, you can go too."

Tommy told Les not to say that, but Les stayed quiet. Kevin suggested that they both take a walk to cool their heads, then come back to relax. Les' body tensed up, but Tommy got his attention and told him it wasn't worth it. Les slammed his fists down at his side then headed out the back door, but not before cursing at Donnie.

Tommy asked that I go and check on Chelsea, then followed Les. When I walked into our store, there was a blanket-covered mass on Chelsea's bed. I called out to her, but there was no response. I pulled the covers off as gently as I could to see her crying body wrapped around the Amy doll.

"I'm so tired of the fighting," she said.

I knew she would've loved to get a grasp on what was happening, but I could tell that she couldn't. I envied her for that. I had her sit up and gave her a tight hug till she stopped crying. I tried to jump down from her bunk, but she grabbed me and asked me not to go. I heard voices coming from the hall, but I couldn't make out what they were saying. I wanted to be part of the conversation, so I told Chelsea that we were going to be strong and go on a patrol together. After a bit of convincing, and after telling her she could bring the doll, she agreed. I told her to guard the entrance to our store and make sure no one snuck in. She seemed happy with that idea, and the serious look on her face as she did it made me smile.

I crept up behind a pillar to listen to what was being said before I could make the decision of storming in or not. Les said that the safety of the mall as a whole was in jeopardy if Donnie remained. Tommy agreed with him, but said they should let him sober up first. Kevin argued that Donnie should stay because of how useful he could be.

The three of them bickered back and forth on what to do while I stayed silent and listened. But then Donnie spoke up.

"I'm fine with leaving," he slurred. "But I'm taking her with me."

All three men had something to say about that, and none were pleased with the idea. They started walking towards him when I came out from behind the pillar. I told them that I agreed with him, and that if he had to go, so did I. They continued to bicker over the issue for a few minutes before Les agreed to wait till the morning to decide.

When I got back to the room, Chelsea told me how good

she'd done at guarding, and I agreed. She did a little spin and jumped back into her bed. I felt a sense of pride from not turning my back on Donnie, even though he was the one who caused all this and probably deserved it. I was positive he wouldn't abandon me like he had Carly. Tommy came over and asked if I was okay, but I hardly registered what he said. Instinctively, I started defending Donnie and saying that he should be allowed to stay, especially since we all knew why he had been acting the way he was. Tommy stopped me and told me to relax. He said he understood, but it needed to be talked about more in the morning.

Les quietly walked in. It took him a while to find the words, but eventually he apologized for saying I could leave. I didn't care and I told him that. The only thing I was worried about was Donnie and helping him get over what he was going through. I explained that if we gave him time, helped him stop drinking, and tried to understand what he'd gone through, maybe he could be himself again.

"That's not going to happen," Les said. "He is an alcoholic... someone who needs to drink to function. He must've gotten clean out of necessity for survival, but now that he's started again, there isn't anything we can do. It's like he never stopped."

His words were heartbreaking, but I said we'd talk about it more in the morning, and he agreed. After Les left, I climbed into Donnie's bunk. I thought that sleeping where he'd slept would give me some sort of comfort, but it didn't. Numbness settled on my bones like an immovable blanket.

My dreams were the same as always: Taylor and her family turning; Georgie sadistically doing things to me; my family getting killed; Rebeca getting killed; everyone saying that everything was my fault. Most nights, these dreams would snap me awake, but not that night. It was like I was looking in on someone else's life, or watching a horror movie. I felt no connection to what I saw. The images all faded to black and there was nothing but void.

"Hey, you gotta get up," Tommy said as he shook me awake. "Was Kevin in here?"

I told him I didn't know. Without pause, he yanked me to my feet and told me that we needed to leave. My eyes were cloudy and wouldn't clear no matter how hard I tried. Then I realized that my eyes weren't cloudy; it was the mall. Smoke was billowing into our store from a glowing fire out in the hall.

CHAPTER 14

Tommy had Chelsea in his arms and we ran for the back door. I said that I needed to get Donnie, but Tommy told me he wasn't there.

"What do you mean?" I asked.

"I don't know where he is, but it looks like he got out from one of the vents in the room."

It was a relief to know that at least Donnie was out. I knew it was a matter of time before he came in to help us get out, so I just needed to hold on till then. We continued running for the back door but stopped when we heard screams for help.

"Damnit," Tommy said as he put Chelsea down next to me. "Get her outside, I'll be back!"

There was no way I was leaving him to do everything himself; it could've been Donnie who needed me. I took Chelsea outside and told her to wait for us there. The gate was locked with a chain and padlock, and no one besides Les and Kevin had a key. I knew she would be safe there just as much as I knew I needed to rush back and help Tommy.

The clouds of smoke danced in the halls like a beautiful ballet and made it impossible to breathe. I fell to my stomach so I could get some air and started crawling towards the cry for help. In the distance, there was someone else on their stomach: it was Les. I called out to him, but he kept low, not moving. I tried getting closer, but I slid and tumbled to my side. I pulled my hand up in front of my face to see what had made me slip and saw the dark blood running down my sleeve. It was pooling around Les' face. I flipped him over and saw that his throat had been slit and a knife wound had been etched into his skull. My body felt hot and started vibrating like I'd been thrown in a dryer. My vision tunneled on his drooped face. The blood glistened shades of red, black, and pink. I placed my hand back into it and felt how refreshing it was, like a warm bath on a cold day. I studied the way it ran down my arm like syrup. I was mesmerized by its beauty.

Another scream for help snapped me out of my daydream and back to what I was there to do. I patted Les down to try and find his keys, but they weren't on him. There was nothing else I could do, so I continued my crawl to whoever needed me.

Fire blazed at the front door and was sneaking its way towards me. A scream echoed from the room with the rock wall. A hue of orange shined under the door as I approached it. Tommy opened the door then shut it behind him. I stood and ran for the door, bursting through and running into Tommy's back.

"Where is Chelsea?" he cried once he heard it was me.

I told him not to worry and that she was safe out in the garden. He didn't seem thrilled with her being alone, but he knew she'd be fine as long as she stayed put.

"We're here!" one voice shouted.

"Please, help us!" another chimed in.

Looking up, I saw Erica and Peter, who had Jillian and Anthony strapped to him. They were at the highest point of the wall, and yelled that they couldn't get the ceiling hatch open. The fire had begun scaling the wall towards them, so there was no way they could climb back down to us. Tommy pointed out that we were limited on time since the fire was covering the door to the ammo room.

"Please forgive us!" Erica yelled, and Peter echoed her.

I asked what it was that they were apologizing for, but Tommy said we should get them down, then ask what they'd done. There were purple mats rolled up next to the wall. I stacked a few of them onto each other, and Tommy helped me pull them under the rock wall.

"Ok!" I shouted, "You have to climb down as far as you can, then you can jump! You'll be fine, we have plenty of mats to break your fall!"

Erica hollered that she was going to start climbing down. It didn't take long for the squeak of her shoes to pierce my ears as she jumped from the wall. Why did she leap like that? Why did she go so far? It was like she wanted to die, but that couldn't have been the case; she loved her family. But then why did she jump so far?

Her body slammed a few feet away from the mats with a thud and crack. There was no point in checking on her. Just looking at the way her head was pinned under her chest was proof enough that she was gone.

"ERICA!" Peter screamed from the top.

I tried telling him that she would be okay, but even through the smoke, I'm sure he could see that she'd landed in an unnatural way. He let out an awful cry, then was silent. I called up to him, but there was nothing except the sound of billowing smoke and crackling fire.

Then there was a short grinding sound from the top, and a dark figure flying towards me. It landed on the ground and bounced twice before coming to rest by Erica. It was Peter. I'm sure he didn't even aim for the mats, just jumped. I approached this body thinking I would see the same snapped neck and pitiful corpse, but Peter had survived. He was still squirming, lying on his face with his arms snapped and his torso spun like a top. Tommy cursed and ran to the wall, saying he needed to get Jillian and Anthony.

I needed to know what Erica and Peter had been apologizing for. Maybe they knew something about Donnie, or what had happened. I rolled him over, then fell to my knees. Jillian and Anthony, his beautiful babies, were still strapped to his chest. I picked up what was left of them in my arms and became transfixed by the mangled flesh and bone. Both their heads were smashed apart like soft-boiled eggs and their blood leaked between my fingers. Tommy shouted down and asked if Peter was okay. I cried for him to come back since the babies were already with me. He was back down in a blink and came over to me. Once he saw what was left of Jillian and Anthony, he started puking over my shoulder.

Strong emotion hadn't been something I was used to lately. Whenever feelings came, they would be a jumbled mess. The first feeling I felt completely again was hatred. It came when I looked back at Peter's pain-filled face. I laid the babies on Erica's chest, then went over to him.

"K-K-Kill me-e..." he begged.

My head rang with the anticipation of being able to see him dead. I patted his pockets and found a set of keys. It may have been my presence which caused it, but Peter seemed calmer with every smoke-filled breath, like he was going to have a peaceful death. That couldn't continue. One of the keys was long and jagged with a sharp tip. He looked at me with fear in his eyes as I placed the key on the center of his throat and pushed. As I laid my weight down, I felt the second true emotion that I had felt in days: joy. His neck hissed and bubbled when there was no more resistance on the key.

"Die," I whispered.

His body started convulsing as it tried drawing air. I stared down at him to watch his eyes go blank, but Tommy ruined my moment. He yanked me out the door as all the ammo caught fire and started exploding.

"You need to go and get Chelsea!" he screamed over the sound of the bullets flying. "I'll go find Kevin or anyone else still here, but please, go protect my girl!"

The more I moved, the more the realization set in that I, again was a murderer, and this time I enjoyed it. A voice in the back of my skull laughed at me. It was so loud and so obnoxious. I screamed at the top of my lungs that I'd heard enough, and a scream that echoed back from inside the mall stopped the laughing.

It sounded like Chelsea and it was coming from our store. I looked inside and found that a Creep had its hand around her mouth as her body thrashed. There was a shattered bottle on the ground so I scooped it up, ran up to the Creep and started stabbing. There was no way this thing was going to turn her. It couldn't. I was right there. The Creep's body started rolling around on the floor before the tar that covered it dissipated.

Chelsea was lying face down and wouldn't move when I called her. The Amy doll was resting on her bed, so I clipped it to my belt and told her she needed to follow to get it back. She still didn't move. I smiled and told her now wasn't the time to play around with me as I flipped her onto her back. Black sludge covered the inside of her mouth. I slammed my fingers into the back of her throat to make her throw up, but there was an opening so large it felt like trying to touch the sides of the ocean. I begged her to look at me just as her eyes sprung open. The beautiful brown of her eyes was offset by the crystal-clear water that started to collect around them. She grabbed me by the shoulder twice as hard as I could grab her and stood to her feet. She started to yawn wider and wider till her cheeks began to tear like paper, as a disgustingly awful creature slithered its way out of her throat. The screaming and crying forced me to look away and cover my ears.

    I knew she had to die. I shrugged off her grip as she swung at me, missing by a mile. I could see the back of her neck. I lunged forward, and just before I plunged the broken bottle into her, I froze. She turned on her heels and smacked me so hard my eyes went crossed. It would've taken me a while to collect myself, but I didn't have the luxury of time.

    "I'm so sorry," I cried as I stood to my feet and stumbled as fast as I could away from her.

    I ran through the back door and into the Puke-infested garden. My eyes were still a foggy mess, but quickly cleared as I noticed one of the monsters that had killed Rebeca standing inside. It stood in front of a peeled-back section of the gate. It stared back at me, taunting me. I took my first step to run, but ended up tumbling down into a hole. Confused, I studied what I'd fallen into and realized it was Rebeca's grave. A trail of black sludge flowed out of it and onto the soil around me. It formed a path that led straight to the monster.

    Rebeca, she was one of them now. She turned into one of those things and was going to kill us all, either her or the monsters she welcomed in with her. I couldn't move a muscle. My mind ached with the thought of her being the one to kill me. Pukes started coming towards the hole, but I wasn't sure that I cared. Maybe being a Puke wouldn't be too bad. Maybe the people cried because the Puke did something to their tear ducts and it wasn't because they were in pain. Maybe we could all be together in some offshoot of heaven until we actually died. Maybe I could live with being dead.

A small voice tickled the back of my ear and Donnie's face popped into my head like the brightest firework. I remembered that he was still out there looking for me, so I couldn't let myself die. I shook off the idea of letting myself become one of them, and made my way around the Pukes. An animalistic roar erupted from Rebeca as I reached the gate. It sent a chill through my body and made me start fumbling with the keys. The fact that the gate was locked and that I'd thought that was a good idea filled me with grief and rage. Running footsteps thudded behind me so I threw my body to the side to avoid the blow. Rebeca smashed into the door and almost threw it from its hinges. All the Pukes were motionless as she turned back to face me. With nowhere else to run, I sprinted back toward the blaze of the mall. The fire was so intense that there was no way I could've entered if I wanted to. I studied the inside, but the archway of the door crumbled down in front of me. Sounds of growling and grinding came from Rebeca as she started getting closer to me.

My mind raced, trying to find a way out, but there was nothing. An idea popped into my head as a smell entered my nostrils. The smell of burning hair and skin reminded me of Les and what he'd told me about these creatures bursting into flames. I picked up a piece of burning wood and looked at Rebeca. She roared again, then charged me. I took a deep breath as I watched and waited. When she was close enough, I stepped out with my right foot, slid my left and used the momentum to twist my hips and stab the fiery wood into her chest.

She started to scream like a vulture and threw her arms around like a windmill. The ground shook when she threw herself down and writhed. I was so mesmerized by her that I almost didn't notice the moan that was coming from my side. I knew something was coming, so I ducked to avoid a blow from one of the Pukes. I darted over to the gate and got the correct key on the first try. It unlocked just as something grabbed hold of me. It was Chelsea, her face one of helplessness and agony. She had to die. Her arm reeled back for a blow that I was able to avoid. I picked up the chain and waited for her to regain her footing. She looked over at me, and I told her I was so sorry as I used my entire body to swing that chain and padlock at her, striking her on the top of her skull. Her head caved in under the pressure of the blow, and the creature slithered out of her mouth and died at my feet.

I felt so sick that I fell to my knees and started gagging on the ground. Gunshots started erupting from behind me and striking the Pukes. I moved as quickly as I could to get away so I wouldn't end up getting hit by a stray bullet. Tommy was the one shooting and he called out for me to move to him, but the Pukes were surrounding me and there was nowhere I could run. I tried shoving one but it hardly moved; instead, its head tore apart.

"Let's go!" Tommy yelled as he pulled me from the swarm.

I started running, but didn't see or hear Tommy behind me. When I checked, he was standing, looking down at the ground. His eyes were dead-set on Chelsea's body. He threw his hands on the top of his head, and started muttering something to himself before letting out a long, painful scream.

Everything turned into a target for his aggression. I ran to him and told him there was nothing we could do, but he didn't pay me any attention. The Pukes were starting to swarm us from every direction and the thought of leaving Tommy to fend for himself festered in my mind.

"You let her die!" he screamed at me. "You let my baby girl

die!"

"I saved her! She turned, so I put her out of her misery! Now, Tommy, we need to move so we don't end up like that too!"

One Puke lunged at me, but I was able to sidestep it and kick out its knees, before Tommy shot it in the back of the head. Then he grabbed a Puke by the throat and threw it on the ground, before crushing its skull with a few stomps. His gun started to click when he pulled the trigger, but he was still smashing the Pukes with it. One of them fell at his feet and slithered up like it was trying to get a look at us. Tommy placed his boot on it and smashed it back down, twisting his foot like he was putting out a cigarette.

There was no end to the Pukes in sight and some Creeps started to show themselves, but Tommy was so focused on fighting that he hardly seemed to realize. Donnie was still waiting for me but I didn't want to leave Tommy behind, so I tried one more time to get him to follow. I grabbed him by the arm and said, "Chelsea wouldn't want you to die like this! She wouldn't want us to die like this!"

As he looked down at me, a Puke grabbed us both and hoisted us into the air. Tommy placed the barrel of the gun against its head, but it only clicked. I kicked it as hard as I could, but that was a lost cause. The Puke started smashing our heads into each other, moaning louder each time. My hearing became muffled as blood pooled in my ear and ran down my face. My vision became dented with black splotches the more we collided. I whispered an apology to Donnie, as I couldn't lift my arms to fight anymore.

A glint of light pierced through my blotched vision. It was the third or fourth smash of our heads when I noticed, and it really bothered me. I was finally getting my completely valid death, and something had to ruin it. I cracked my eyes open to the size of a penny slot, and that's when I saw a folding knife sticking out of the Pukes shoulder. It reminded me of the one I'd lost when I was still with Donnie, and all the times he'd saved me. I wanted to try just a little harder for him since he was the only family I had left.

Since my arms were too heavy to lift, I threw my legs up with all my might. That was supposed to be enough to get myself free, but it only made the Puke squeeze harder. I knew I was going to black out if I didn't do something, so I leaned my body back with all the strength I had left, and slammed my foot down onto the blade. The Puke finally dropped me, by which point the only vision I had left was the size of a pinhole. My neck burned, but I pushed the feeling away and stood as quickly as my body would let me.

The Puke swung Tommy at me, forcing me to dive to the ground. Tommy was a pale blue and looked like he was already dead. I posted my hands and one foot on the ground, then with my free foot, I smashed through the Puke's kneecap, causing it to tumble to the ground. It released Tommy so it could stand, and the color started returning to his face. That gave me some hope, determined that we could actually make it out alive. With my right hand, I pulled the knife free from the Pukes shoulder before it could get to its feet. With my left hand, I held its head to the ground. The creature began circling around the back of the human's head and pointed at me. I smiled as I slid the blade into the nape of the neck and listened to this thing hiss as it died.

I placed the knife in my back pocket before I went to check on Tommy. He was unconscious, but I didn't have the pleasure of time to wake him nicely. I smacked him until he took a deep inhale. His eyes were like glass, and they darted around everywhere like he was trying to take everything in at once. I made him sit up and said that we needed to move. I tried placing his arm around my shoulder but he cried out in pain when I moved it. The shoulder was clearly dislocated, but we didn't have time for pity. I told him to take a breath in and out. As soon as he started to exhale, I wrapped his arm around me and helped him to his feet. He was so heavy, and the fact that he was squirming in pain made it so hard to move with him. That pain turned out to be a blessing since it was so overwhelming that it snapped him from his daze. He pushed me to the side and looked at me with firm eyes, saying he was good to run on his own. I yelled for him to prove it as we ran into the dense brush of the woods.

CHAPTER 15

The sun started setting as we trudged through sticker bushes and poison ivy. The sounds of Pukes still permeated through the dusk air. Tommy started to lag behind, so in a sorry attempt to motivate him, I told him that we had to keep moving. Before he could take another step, he collapsed on the ground. His lips were the same shade of white as his face and his whole body shook. I pulled up his sleeve to see that his arm had turned black and blue; the only thing keeping it attached to his body was elastic skin.

I tried keeping him calm by saying that he was fine, but I knew that if we kept moving through the night, he'd not be able to continue at all. I didn't want to have gone through all that turmoil at the mall just to have him end up dead a few miles away. He looked down at his arm then at me, his expression a mix of fear and determination.

"You're going to have to set it," he grunted.

He gingerly placed himself flat on the ground and instructed me to put my foot on his chest and pull his arm to the sky. With no other option, I did what he asked. He squirmed on the ground as he tried finding the correct angle to reset his shoulder. Eventually it worked and his arm let out a deep pop as he sighed with relief. I tore a piece of cloth from his shirt and fashioned a makeshift sling to keep his arm from swinging. We decided to huddle underneath a fallen tree and rest for the night.

"Can I have that?" Tommy asked.

I looked to see what he was asking for and saw the Amy doll

on my hip. I unclipped it and handed it over without a word. He whispered a meek 'thanks' then rolled away from me. His shoulders started to bounce as he carefully curled himself around the doll.

Sleep didn't grace me that night, but I'd expected that. I was so focused on finding Donnie that I knew I had to keep my guard high. I needed to get out of the woods, so I needed to stay alive, and to do that, I needed to stay aware. At first light, I shook Tommy, but he was already awake. He asked if he could keep the doll with him, and since it would be better in his hands than mine, I had no issue.

We marched out of the woods after a few more hours of walking and ended up in a small town. The streets, made of cracked brick, had given way to plant life, which exploded through the paths. Tommy wasn't talking much and I figured it would be best not to push him. There was a house that looked to still be in good shape, and the possibility of supplies inside made my mouth water. Of course, the front door was locked, so I told Tommy to search one side of the home for an entrance, while I searched the other. He stopped me, took a step back and smashed his boot through the front door.

"Found our way in," he said.

The inside of the house was beautiful, featuring a fireplace, furniture with the odd rip, and hardwood floors that hadn't splintered. The only thing that reduced the house's value was the air, which was filled with mold and the smell of two dead bodies. They were holding hands, but each arm had slices up and down them, and they both had a hole in the back of their head. A massive, drippy heart was drawn on the wall behind them, like one last symbol of their love.

They were people who'd felt so privileged that they'd taken

themselves out just so they didn't need to suffer like the rest of us. Why did they get to die but I was still here? I'd been fine with death taking me away many times, but I'd always been forced to find a reason to keep going. They'd taken the easy way out, and I told Tommy that. His face was blank after I spoke.

"It's not... easy. It's very far from that," he answered, looking down at the doll cradled in his sling.

We decided to search the house, and found some canned foods and even some fresh water. A scratchy, wooden door stood at the back of the house. When I opened it, there was nothing but a set of stairs going down and darkness. I felt my face flush as I tried to muster up courage to enter a room like that again, but Tommy did it for me. I was embarrassed, but I tried not to let it show too much. He came back up after a few minutes and said everything was clear.

Tommy said it would be best if we stayed there for the rest of the day and that night to make sure that we weren't being followed. I agreed because Tommy needed the rest, but I knew Donnie was still looking for me. He wouldn't give up searching, but it almost felt like betrayal to take a night off from looking for him.

Tommy and I dragged the bodies outside and gave them an impromptu burial. We covered them with some leaves and a few rocks stacked at their heads. I told Tommy to head back inside to rest.

"I've rested plenty," he said. "You go in and clear out that fireplace so we can get a fire going with the sticks we collect."

I asked who he meant when he said 'we.' He twisted with a painful-looking smile before lifting his arm and revealing the Amy doll. I smiled back at him and told him to stay safe, then I headed back inside to clean up our new home. He needed rest, but he could also use time to himself.

About an hour ticked by and Tommy hadn't returned. There was a massive window facing the front yard that I looked out through. The sun hadn't started to set, but it was getting close. Deer, fox, rabbits and squirrels were all running together in the wonderland of brick and plants. One of the deer was beautiful. It had chestnut fur with a slightly paler underbelly. It must've been young since it still had the funniest outline of white spots littering its body. I studied how graceful and streamlined it was so intently that I almost forgot about the world.

One second the deer was eating, the next it flipped its tail and ran, and so did the rest of the animals. Even though my picture-perfect view was gone, I was glad to see Tommy walking back towards the house. He had a limp and was dragging something large at his side, but I couldn't quite make it out. I ran to help him pull whatever he was dragging, but stopped when I noticed it moving. The closer he got, the more he started to take shape. This man wasn't Tommy. It was my nightmare resurrected. It was Georgie.

"Hello, beautiful," he said, in a way that made my bones chatter like windchimes. "I think we can make a deal: you come with me, I set him free."

He lifted what was dragging at his side and revealed that it was Tommy. Fear and anger rushed through my body like an electrical current. I knew I needed to keep as calm as possible to help Tommy, so I stood motionless.

"Listen to me, Alex," Georgie yelled as he reached behind his back. "You are going to come out here, and you are going to give me a big, wet kiss. Then, you're going to say how sorry you are for leaving me." He pulled out a butcher's knife. "And if you don't, I'm going to slit your friend's throat and pull his tongue through the hole."

There was nothing I could do but comply. All the blood in my body seemed to drop from my head into my legs, pinning me to the ground and making me feel like passing out. I threw my hands into the air to show how submissive I was going to be.

"That's the good girl I remember. Now come here and show me how you've grown."

He walked up to me, pulling Tommy, a struggling heap, with him, and wrapped me in his arms. Tommy's sling was being used as a tie for his hands and the Amy doll was stuffed deep into his mouth.

"Don't be a rude little bitch… hug me," he demanded after I didn't embrace him back.

My arms were led as I lifted and wrapped them around Georgie's waist. He smiled and pulled me in close so I could smell his odor of dirt, blood, and sweat. He started running his fingers through my hair, stopping occasionally to give it a slight tug. He seemed happy when my expression turned to one of pain.

We were going to die; I was sure of that. Maybe not a physical death, but my soul was already carrying a cross up a hill. If Georgie took us, I'd be nailed to it. My knife was still in my back pocket and I knew that I'd be quick enough to slit his throat if I could get my hands around it. Gingerly, I moved my hand down his body until it was parallel with me again, then started to bend it to reach into my pocket.

"Now, now, Alex. Is that the smartest thing for you to do?" Georgie said, realizing what I was doing and snatching my arm, pulling it into the air.

Tommy sat up and kicked Georgie's knees, throwing him off balance. I pulled away from him, popped open my knife and took a stab at his skull, but only managed to cut his chin. He grabbed me again and pulled my knife away, but I was able to scurry and run back into the house.

Georgie let out a long exhale and pulled Tommy to his feet.

I hollered for him to let Tommy go and that we would be able to figure something out. The tremble in my voice as I spoke filled me with disgust and self-loathing. It was like I had my tough-girl face on but was still the same weak, useless child that Georgie had made his.

"You don't need to put on an act with me... I know you, and I know you need me," he said.

He told me to come out and that he would make it easy for all of us. That I'd be safe with him, and I wouldn't need to be worried ever again so long as I listened. This time, before I spoke, I cleared my throat and snapped that those things would never be allowed to happen to me again.

"Okay..." he said with a shrug, placing the knife against Tommy's throat.

The realization hit me that he would leave Tommy alone if he had me. I could tell Tommy to go find Donnie, and they could both come save me. I didn't know how long I could last with Georgie, but if I knew they were alive and coming, I'd be able to suffer through.

"Wait!" I pleaded as I walked back out to him.

He demanded I turn my pockets out to show him I didn't have another weapon, so I did. Tommy was still standing, but Georgie put him on the ground before coming to me. He caressed my face with his hand before pulling it back and slapping me with it.

"That there are consequences for your actions is a concept you clearly don't understand... I'm going to change that," he said, wiping the blood trickling from his chin. "You know how many people died because you were so selfish? If you'd listened and done what I asked for a few more weeks, all this would have been resolved, and we would have a society again."

Tommy was behind Georgie, making eye contact with me. My glances over Georgie's shoulder were brief, since I was trying to tell him everything would be okay if we relaxed. He didn't get the message. His face contorted into a whirlpool of pain as he slipped his hands free of the binding and started creeping up. My mind raced, trying to find a way to make him stop without alerting Georgie, but all I could do was stare and hope everything could work out. He grabbed Georgie's shoulder, spun him around like a top and threw his body weight behind a punch. It was a grazing blow that only staggered Georgie. He brought his knife up to slash Tommy, but I jumped and grabbed his arm, throwing the knife to the ground. He paid me back with a punch to the stomach that took every ounce of energy out of me. I flopped to the floor, trying to contain the pain radiating through me. Georgie grabbed Tommy's injured arm and yanked it behind him, causing it to make a loud pop.

"You fucking assholes!" Georgie screamed over Tommy's painful moans.

He drew a gun from under his shirt and held it to the back of Tommy's head. I finally caught my breath and pleaded with him not to kill Tommy.

"I'm going to make you understand obedience…" he said with a smile.

Bodies don't fall like you'd think when their shot. It's not a graceful and slow motion. It's fast and embarrassing. That's how Tommy's body fell when his thoughts were splattered all over me. It got in my eyes and mouth. It tasted like sour candy.

Georgie started coming for me, but I ran away, back inside the house. My body wouldn't stop trembling as I ran to the wooden door. I started creeping down the steps when Georgie burst into the house. He started taunting me like it was a game of hide and seek. My footsteps became quiet and deliberate. Every time a creek rang out through the floor, I'd stop dead and wait.

"I've come all this way to keep you safe," he said. "When I asked Erica and Peter to light the mall up so I could draw you out, they did it without question. They understood the safety I can offer if you just listen to me. Why can't you be more like your friends, Erica and Peter?"

Erica and Peter's apologies made sense now. It only made me happier at the thought of their corpses burning. My steps landed me in the middle of the basement. The white walls looked like a Rorschach painting with all the black mold. The floor was littered with boxes, cinder blocks, and empty booze bottles. I guessed the people who'd been upstairs had wanted to go out after a party.

Georgie's thumping footsteps got closer to the basement steps as I found a pair of storm doors. As quietly as I could, I sprinted up to them, slid the latch, and pushed each side open. Each creak that the heavy, metal doors let out was a beat my heart skipped. I prayed for Georgie to be momentarily deaf, or better yet, permanently. After a few seconds that felt like hours of pushing open the doors, they started making an odd noise. Not a grinding or jagged movement, but a groaning and moaning. A shadow started peeking through the door as it finally opened. A Puke was waiting for me on the other side, seemingly wanting to play hide and seek with me too, and it had just won.

It reached its hands forward and grabbed a hold of my shirt, but I slammed one of the doors down on its arms and stumbled out of the way. There was a thin sheet of metal posted up against the side of the stairs, and I took what little time I had left to huddle under it. The Puke lost sight of me as it flung the door open and came down into the basement. The force it opened the doors with caused both of them to bounce back and slam closed. I hated this Puke. Not only had it just taken away my escape, but it had told Georgie where I was. This Puke was old too. It walked with a limp and only let out weak noises of pain every few steps, so I could tell this body was about to die.

When I first looked around in the basement, I thought that

the size would work for me; it was big and open, lots of space to move around if I needed to. Now that openness was my enemy as the Puke wandered out of sight, and by now, Georgie had made his way down.

"I know you're here…" Georgie said in a loud whisper that cut through me.

I couldn't have lived with myself if I rolled over and died. Not while I still needed to find Donnie. Trying to motivate myself to do something, I wiped some of Tommy's blood off my face and studied it. The harder chunks were mixed in with squishy ones, and they all wandered around in the deep, red fluid. I started to become entranced by it, but a shine from a bottle that laid a few feet from me grabbed my attention instead.

Georgie was in front of me, carefully moving things aside so he wouldn't alert me until he wanted to. He hadn't seen the Puke yet, and it hadn't found him. Gripping the bottle with all the courage I had left, I poked my head up a bit from the metal sheet and whispered to Georgie.

"Oh!" he exclaimed. "Hello, beautiful."

I took the bottle and threw it as hard as I could, smashing it against his chest. He cursed at me as he wiped his chest clear of broken glass fragments.

"That's it, you little bitch!" he yelled. "I'm going to fucking kill you!"

He started marching over to me, and I ducked back down a little bit behind the metal sheet. He drew his gun and pointed it at me, but before he could act, the Puke showed itself from around the corner.

"I'll let you die and suffer like you deserve," he said with a smile.

The Puke mustered new energy, now making its human host moan and cry loudly. It got close to me, and that made Georgie smile with glee as he waited to watch me die. I stared back with a smile to match his as the creature brushed its hand over my hair and reached for Georgie.

He jumped back with surprise, tripping over one of the boxes he'd just moved. The Puke grabbed him and smashed his face with all its might, sending him tumbling to the ground. It turned Georgie on his back and seemed to give him mouth to mouth. His body writhed like it was falling down a pit. His gun slid out of his hand, and I ran to it. The moment was so satisfying; he looked at me as if I'd help him, reaching out his arms for me to pull him away. So funny. So cute.

Once the Puke was done, it wasn't hard to kill it with only a few shots to the body. Georgie stood, clutching his stomach, then looked at me with pure anger. He ran at me with both arms outstretched, but he stumbled when he got close. He looked down at himself, then back up at me with an expression of pure pain and despair. I laughed as his jaw slammed to his chest and the writhing tar snapped itself up from deep within his stomach. Tears flowed down his face like a river, and in that moment, I couldn't have been happier. I slowly made my way to the storm doors, finding ecstasy in Georgie's pain.

"Now suffer…" I said as I slammed the heavy doors closed and locked him in there to rot.

CHAPTER 16

Tommy's body was sprawled out on the front lawn. I walked up to him, half expecting him to jump back to his feet and tell me what to do next. I mourned him along with any love I had left for myself. He'd died because of me. Chelsea had died because of me. If I had died instead, they'd still be alive, or at least I wouldn't have had to see them die.

I noticed a small, stuffed foot sticking out from under Tommy. I rolled him onto his back, exposing his mangled face. It was so deep, yet so shallow. The hole made him look like a blooming flower, ready to be plucked. The only thought that came to me was how clean and pure it was. How we all look like that on the inside. How beautiful it all looked. I placed my finger inside the hole and studied its dimensions. I pulled some of his skin to try and cover it back up to see if that would make him look any better, but it didn't work. A part of his skin tore from his skull and I studied that next. The way it jiggled in my hands and how weightless it was. I could stretch it and squish it, but it would always return to the same shape.

The more I studied the skin, the more a buzzing filled my ears. I didn't mind it at first, but then it started to hurt. I wanted to put the skin down and cover my ears, but it was just so beautiful. I thought about matching it with a piece of my own. The ringing grew but I needed to match this skin with mine, so I blocked it out. A sound similar to a drum's beat started to join the buzzing. The closer my hands got to my head, the louder the drum got. I gently laid my fingers on my head and started scraping down. The drums were so loud in my head, but I needed to match him. The drums are so loud.

"STOP!" a voice shouted.

I looked around, but there was no one I could see. I knew I needed to move, so I threw away the skin and picked up the Amy doll. Before I left Tommy, I made him a promise: to keep the doll safe with me for as long as I could.

Finding Donnie was my main priority, but I had no idea where he would've gone. With no better idea, I headed south since that had been our plan at the very beginning. I stuck to the road, not wanting to go back into the woods unless I needed to. The night was quickly approaching and I truly did not want to spend a night in the wild alone. Unfortunately for me, that was not a decision I had the pleasure of making. The sun's warmth left as it set behind the decrepit trees of the wood line. I found a house that had completely fallen to the ground, but there was a shed in the back that was perfect for me to spend the night in. There was a bent coat hanger that held the door closed, but I unbent it and kept it with me in case something got stuck in the barrel of my gun. I made a hole just outside the door and started a fire inside it. I didn't have much with me anymore, but what I did carry I placed on the ground and laid down next to it.

Silence can be so incredibly soothing at times, but horrifically unsettling at others. I'd close my eyes and see Rebeca's decapitated skull, Les' slit throat, Erica's contorted body, and Tommy's mangled face. Their deaths filled me with grief to the point where I wanted to cry, but even when I tried to, it was like I'd forgotten how. Everything was numb. Nothingness. A void. Falling deeper into my thoughts was the only thing I was willing to do. The more I thought, the more I didn't feel. Nothing is like silence, and it was becoming horrifically soothing to me.

"Hey!" a voice yelled to me, shocking me with its abruptness.

I sprung to my feet, grabbed my gun, and waited for whoever it was to show themselves. No one came; there was just the crackling warmth of the fire. Keeping my eyes fixed on the world outside the door, I slowly placed my gun back on the floor. Once I let it go, it tumbled a bit before coming to a rest. I realized I'd set it on top of the Amy doll, leaving a black smudge across its face. I cleaned it as best I could, but there was still a bit of residue left behind. Feeling bad for her, I held her in my arms and rested my body on the splintery wooden floor.

My gaze was still focused on looking outside, but my eyes were so heavy that I couldn't do anything to keep them open anymore. When they closed, I saw things that made me feel again. I felt... happy? I wasn't happy like I'd used to be before all of this happened. It was more like when you eat a sour candy or bite into your favorite food when it's missing one important ingredient. It was harsh around the edges, but sweet at its core. It was good to have but far from being perfect.

I thought of Tommy and Chelsea's hugs, Donnie's gentle smile, Les' awkward way of speaking, and Rebeca's talks with me. All things I cherished now, in my memory, but hadn't nearly enough when I'd had them at my disposal. Those thoughts slowly faded for even better ones, ones that I had no regret for. The thought of terror gripping Georgie as his jaw ripped away from his skull. The thought of sliding the sharp key into Peter's throat to disturb his undeserving attempt at a peaceful death. In those thoughts lay the happiness I remembered. The happiness that was pure, and that I wasn't ashamed to feel.

The birds singing in the morning were my signal to wake up and continue moving. I slid my gun into the back of my belt, but I held the Amy doll close to my chest. Having it there made me feel better about finding Donnie; I was hopeful and it felt nice. I walked a few miles and snuck past a few Pukes before I found anything. In the distance, there was a house with smoke billowing from the chimney. My hopes weren't high since anyone could've been there, but it was still worth searching.

CHAPTER 17

My toes curled with glee when I got to the house and saw Donnie's backpack placed outside the front door. I rushed towards it, not caring about my surroundings. I was going to have my best friend with me again, the only one that I had left. The door was locked, so with foolish joy, I screamed that he needed to let me in. Pukes started to flock from the surrounding houses. There was a small mail slot that I lifted and saw the house was completely dark except for the glow of a burning fire. I shouted in for Donnie, but there was still no response. Pukes were getting closer by the second, so I needed to figure out a way inside. I made the already distorted coat hanger into a hook and slid it through the mail slot. It latched round the handle and flipped open the door. I grabbed Donnie's bag, ran inside, and slammed the door shut on the approaching Pukes.

The house was surprisingly nice. Bright pink walls surrounded old timey furniture, which hadn't been torn apart too badly yet. I shouted for Donnie again, but there was still no response. He'd never have left his bag outside if he wasn't still there. I left my gun and Amy on one of the couches, then started to look around. Behind a set of swinging doors was a staircase that led to an upper floor. My heart must've skipped five beats when I saw Donnie's shadow swaying in one of the doorways. I threw myself up the stairs, skipping as many steps as my feet would allow me to. I reached the door, flung my body around the corner and saw Donnie. His mouth hung open. His eyes were a pus yellow color. His neck was stretched away from his levitating body. Donnie was hanging.

I whispered his name, but he didn't respond. I was frozen where I stood, glued to the ground as his lifeless eyes seemed to focus on me. My knees gave up and I landed on my face. I wanted to break down or weep to get it out, but I couldn't. My body wouldn't do it. A few tears were freed and allowed to run down my cheeks, but that was all there was. I sat up, smashed my fist into the ground so something would radiate through me again. I started studying Donnie and I could tell he hadn't been there long. Only a few hours or a day at the most.

A scream startled me as it echoed in the house. I didn't move to check who or what it was. I was too busy with Donnie. The scream kept getting louder and more panicked, but I didn't care. Eventually, it was all around me and deep inside my ears. I closed my eyes and focused on where it was coming from, and realized it was me.

I was screaming, crying, and my face was contorted with pain. It was a shock to me. I didn't remember when I started to cry, but once I knew it was me, I couldn't stop it. I stayed there, not moving from that spot for an entire day screaming with emotions that I couldn't feel anymore. I was along for the ride my body wanted to go on.

As the sun started to rise, my stomach finally began to relax, after a night filled with pushing and contracting. Donnie still hung above me. His face had turned a grayish white, and what I could see of his lower body was a plumb purple. I stood, trembling like a leaf as I walked over to him. I gave him a poke to make sure it wasn't a prank I hadn't caught onto yet. The straining of the rope as he swung let me know it was real. All I craved was an answer as to why he'd thought this was the best idea. How could he have been such a coward when he knew I was coming to find him? How could he leave me just as easily as everyone else? I was still stuck in this shithole world, constantly cheated out of my turn to die. It made my stomach turn as I realized I was over it all.

I walked downstairs to find my gun and the Amy doll, then meandered back up. Donnie's feet banged against my stomach as I made him swing. I wondered if he'd felt like I did now before he jumped. There was a small step stool by his feet that I picked up and stood on, then placed the gun to my head. The method may have been different, but the result would be the same as his. I closed my eyes, took the tension out of the trigger, then squeezed.

Click... click.

The gun was empty. I fell from the stool, clutching my chest and trembling. My body was a wreck and it took a long time before I crawled back to my feet. As I did, I came face to face with a crumpled piece of paper with some writing on it.

I've never felt this way before. So much failure rests on me. Erica and Peter came inside and lit a fire at the front of the mall. Les went to them and Erica killed him. She threw the knife before running to the wall. My only regret is not being able to kill them... That isn't my only regret. Carly was just like Alex. I should have saved them. When I went back, the fire was so fucking high, I couldn't pass it to get to her... I couldn't save another daughter. Kevin found me, gave me my stuff. I tried to bring him back to help but he said it was a lost cause. He said I couldn't focus on what was already lost. No, no, I can't do that. I'm no good at all. I picked up the drink to forget Carly's face, but it only made me lose another. The drink does nothing now except make me realize what I know I need to do. My only hope is that my sorry soul sees my daughters again.

The paper was stained with a bit of blood, soot, and tears. What a fool he'd been. A damned stupid fool. Everything was gone: my parents, the mall, Rebeca, Tommy, Chelsea, and now Donnie. The gun was back against my skull as I pulled the trigger, praying for a bullet to manifest in the barrel. I wanted to be gone too, but I was apparently cursed to stay. I refused.

I brought Donnie's bag up and looked through it for something to use. All the empty bottles he used to have were gone, except for a single glass one. After smashing it on the ground, there was a beautifully large and sharp piece of glass. Squeezing the newly made blade filled me with such anticipation that I sliced open my hand. The warmth of the fresh cut started to run along my wrist. I felt a sense of relief and release. It was the best I'd felt in a long time.

"Hey, Alex," a voice said, but no one was around.

I looked to Donnie to see if he was talking, but his tongue was hanging out of his mouth and bit in two. The voice spoke again and said the same greeting. I scurried to the stairs and looked down, but nothing was there.

"Hey, Alex," it said again and was so close, it was like they were standing next to me.

"What?" I shouted.

Then there was silence. I started sliding the blade up my arm again, getting dizzy from the sight of my blood, but I knew what I had to do. The silence abruptly ended as the voice started screaming my name again.

"WHAT DO YOU WHAT FROM ME?" I was forced to scream as I tried making every sound stop.

"For starters, you can put the glass down, kiddo," the voice said. "After you do that, look at me."

No one was there, so with a tremble on my voice, I asked where I should look.

"Down here."

It told me which way to walk, then just before I took another step, it shouted for me to stop. I looked down and the Amy doll was resting at my feet.

"Hi," she said without moving.

Her voice changed a few times from masculine, to soft, then to another slightly masculine voice. They all blended together and formed a single tone before I asked who she was.

"Well, it's us silly: Chelsea, Donnie, and Tommy."

My eyes were overcome with tears as I scooped them into my arms. They told me to wait to hold them and to go through Donnie's bag for bandages, so that's what I did. A flap of skin started to fall off my arm, but I didn't care. I threw it back into place and wrapped it up. Nothing was going to keep my attention away from the doll. I turned back to see that they were sitting against a wall and watching me.

"So, you guys can move?" I asked.

"Not entirely sure yet, but maybe?"

I smiled and held them to my chest when they said how happy they were to be around me again. The only problem was, I was never sure who was speaking. They told me to address all of them as Amy. I told them they were all dead, but they laughed and said they couldn't leave me feeling so alone. We spent the night together and all I did was listen to them talk about how they were so happy to be with me. I was overjoyed, I refused to blink. They couldn't leave my sight for a second.

As the sun rose, Amy suggested we leave. My cheeks were cramping from my smile, which obscured my vision. I jumped to my feet and grabbed them. We got to the ground floor and I threw everything I had into Donnie's bag.

"Let's head south… That was the plan at the start, wasn't it?" Amy asked, and I agreed.

For the first time in as long as I could remember, I was excited about traveling. It had seemed terrifying to go all that way before, but now I had my family with me again. They told me they'd never leave me, and I knew they were right.

The world holds a newfound charm for me. Life is worth living again. So wherever I go, I know I don't need to be alone. That's enough for me.

Printed by BoD"in Norderstedt, Germany